# Murder, Mystery & Mothers

A Willowcroft Cozy Mystery Book One

Fran Heap

This is a work of fiction. The characters, locations, businesses, events and incidences are products of the author's imagination. Any resemblance to actual persons living or dead, or actual events is purely coincidental.

First published by Frances Heap contactable at fran@franheapwriter.com

A catalogue record for this book is available from the National Library of Australia

Cover design by 100Covers.

Created with Atticus

# Willowcroft Gazette

WILLOWCROFT TOWNSHIP WEEKLY NEWS    Since 1926    no. 5088    **27th April, 2025**

# CHARMING LITTLE BLUE COTTAGE FOR SALE

**REPRINT FROM "REALTY PRESS"**
**By Arthur Doyle**

In the picturesque town of Willowcroft, Michigan, a hidden gem awaits you at 7 Cedar Lane. Known affectionately by the locals as the "little blue cottage," this property embodies the quintessential charm of small-town America. With its pale blue exterior standing out amidst lush greenery, this home offers a perfect blend of cozy comfort and natural beauty.

Stepping through the white picket fence, you are greeted by a beautifully maintained garden, where the air is filled with the sweet fragrances of lilacs and elderflowers. The garden is a peaceful haven, ideal for morning coffees or afternoon reading sessions on the porch. The melodic sound of wind chimes provide a gentle background to the serene setting.

Willowcroft is a place where time seems to slow, offering a peaceful respite from the hustle and bustle of modern life. The cobblestoned town square is home to a collection of charming businesses that make everyday life a delight. Just a short stroll from the cottage, you'll find the beloved Swinging Spoon diner, a local favorite where the coffee is always hot and the bacon is fried to perfection. The town also boasts a delightful bakery, known for its freshly baked breads and apple pies.

For those who appreciate a good read or a touch of nostalgia, the local bookstore and antique store offer treasures waiting to be discovered. The bookstore, with its cozy nooks and crannies, is an ideal spot for losing yourself in a novel, while the antique store provides a fascinating glimpse into the past with its unique collection of curiosities.

The little blue cottage is more than just a charming home; it's a gateway to a community rich with character and convenience. The town is nestled between the whispering pines of a nearby state park and the serene expanse of hilly green pastures, providing a picturesque backdrop for your new life. The surrounding area offers a wealth of outdoor activities, from hiking rugged trails through oak, maple, and pine forests to enjoying a peaceful evening at the local drive-in, where you can watch classic movies under the stars.

The property extends to include some of the surrounding paddocks, offering a touch of rural charm and ample space for gardening or simply enjoying the open air. The neighborhood itself is a tranquil enclave, where the quiet hum of crickets fills the evening air and friendly neighbors are always ready with a warm greeting.

Owning the little blue cottage is more than just purchasing a property; it's embracing a lifestyle filled with simplicity, beauty, and a deep connection to nature. If you're seeking a home where you can enjoy the tranquility of a quaint town, the adventure of nearby rugged trails, and the joy of a close-knit community, then 7 Cedar Lane is the perfect place for you. Don't miss the chance to make this little piece of paradise your own.

THE NEW SWINGING SPOON DINER MENU ON PAGE 7

# Chapter 1

At three in the morning, with her cursor blinking on an empty page, Tammy Rumbelow stumbled upon an online listing in rural Michigan. For the first time in months, a flicker of hope sparked.

The realtor's photos of the little blue cottage with its front porch and white picket fence, had set her heart alight. The interior was as enchanting as the exterior, featuring an antique writing desk where inspiration could strike.

On a whim—or perhaps out of desperation—she'd picked up the phone and bought it based on the pictures alone. She had never even visited the state before. Had fate handed her a lifeline, or had she made the biggest mistake of her life?

Now, six weeks later, Tammy's fingers tightened around the steering wheel; nerves and fanfare clashed in her stomach. This was it—her fresh start. But a familiar undercurrent of doubt threatened to bubble to the surface. She turned off the highway. The country roads, flanked by dense forests of oak, maple, and pine, marked the last stretch of her six-day drive from Los Angeles to Willowcroft.

She rolled down the window. The crisp breeze tousled long, wavy strands of brown hair over her face. Tammy inhaled, savoring the clean air. It reminded her of childhood summers—when life was untangled.

As the miles stretched behind her, the hum of the tires a constant companion, fragments of her former life in LA surfaced. Tammy's chest constricted at the memory of her best manuscript—a boundary-pushing idea. But she'd never seen it in print, at least not under her name. Instead, her rushed, uninspired replacement made it to the shelves, the one cobbled together in the aftermath, her creativity fractured and trust shattered.

The book reviews rang in her head. "No emotional depth." "Lacked soul." Tammy winced, acknowledging their bitter truth. But the one that stung the deepest: "She's not just over forty, she's over, full stop." *They don't know the real story behind those pages.*

"You can never do anything right," her mother's sneer boomed, reopening old wounds. It had taken years to quiet the nagging doubts from her childhood, but the betrayal let those words flood back stronger than ever. The steering wheel grew slick under her clammy palms.

A road sign came into view, providing a diversion. "Welcome to Willowcroft. Township Population 999. Greater Willowcroft Population 5,124."

*Will I tip the scales to an even thousand?* Any distraction helped. Was two thousand miles far enough away to break free?

As she entered the town, the street opened into a charming square, its surface covered with cobblestones. Colorful awnings over stores and cafés lined the edges, and the smell of baking pastries hovered in the air. Her gaze drifted upward and to the right, where a clock tower rose above the rooftops, its weathervane catching the sunlight. At its base, a wooden sign marked a branching road: "Willowcroft State Park—Entrance Ahead." It disappeared into a wall of trees, their dense canopy hinting at the forest's depth.

On her left, a bookstore caught her attention. The large bay window displayed her mystery series—evidence of what she'd once achieved. Pride and pain tangled in her chest. Those books represented who she'd been before her life was rewritten without her consent. And before the doubt allowed her mother's words to seep back in.

The town clock chimed, startling Tammy from her reverie. She'd stopped in the middle of the road. No cars honked. Sundays, it seemed, were quiet in Willowcroft. Shaking off her daze, she checked the GPS—7 Cedar Lane was a few minutes away.

The town faded into green meadows. Mature trees dotted the landscape, and a glittering stream wove through the countryside. Tammy's breath caught as she pulled her sedan up to the little blue cottage. It was more beautiful than the photos, despite its weathered paint. Flowers ran along the fence, their summery fragrance filling the air.

Tammy stepped out and stretched her driving-weary body. Awe and trepidation swirled as she took in the place she would now call home. This was it: her reboot. The haunted motel on Route 66 flashed into her mind, with its flickering neon sign and whispers in the walls. Solving that mystery had helped rekindle her creativity. Would the inspiration last?

She walked toward the gate, which creaked as it opened. The garden was lush with greenery and color. The porch stairs groaned under her feet as she climbed. What secrets would they spill if they could talk?

A sign in cheerful script hung on the door. "Welcome Home, Tammy!"

The simple gesture produced a tear. Maybe her mom was wrong. She wiped at the drop. *Or maybe they just haven't met me yet.*

Wind chimes sang above her, their melody a counterpoint to her mother's voice. She needed to learn to trust again, not just others, but her own instincts. Time to work on silencing her mom's voice while amplifying her own.

She turned the doorknob.

Tammy's heart skipped as she crossed the threshold into her new life. An earthy scent tickled her nose as she explored the living room. The wooden floor squeaked underfoot as her fingers brushed the velvety arm of a well-worn chair. She paused in front of the fireplace, her palm resting on the cool, solid hearthstone. Its rough texture anchored her to the moment. She pictured winter evenings reading by its orange glow.

The creak of the floorboards followed her into the kitchen. The old-fashioned stove stood like a relic of simpler times, its metal surface gleaming. The thought of yeast rising in warm dough teased her senses, the imagined aroma almost real. Her fingers itched to rediscover the joy of bringing a recipe to life.

The bedroom beckoned next, its patchwork quilt drawing her in. She ran her hand over its uneven squares. *Does each handsewn piece have a story?* In the corner, a small writing desk invited her to sit, open a notebook, and pour herself onto the page.

"Ahhh." The sanctuary she'd been searching for. *But will it be enough?*

Tammy moved to the window. The silhouette of the quaint town center, with its prominent main square and clock tower, came into view. Sounds of the countryside drifted in—the twittering of birds and the swishing of grass. A world away from the relentless traffic noise and sirens in LA.

She looked up, imagining stars sparkling in the dark, unspoiled by city lights. A dog's bark brought her back to the present. *Is this where I'll find my happiness?*

Her fingers skimmed the walls as she returned to the living room. The empty shelves waited to be filled with her belongings and new memories. Old wounds wouldn't heal just because she'd crossed state lines, but she had to try. Time to unpack.

She reached into a packing box, finding her dog-eared copy of *The Misplaced Motive*—her debut novel. A runaway success. The Tammy from then could never have imagined her situation now. She traced its spine before placing it on the shelf beside her gran's vintage Agatha Christie collection.

Next came the photo of her and Sally at their college graduation, but she returned it to the box. She was not ready to remember the good times with the bad times still fresh.

Tammy's shoulders slumped. Six days of driving had caught up with her. Her hands trembled as she filled a kettle. Earl Grey—her comfort tea. The one constant through every upheaval.

Tammy kicked off her shoes and curled up on the sofa. She sank into the well-worn cushions, her earlier doubts lingering, but softened by the cottage's coziness. Here, away from the recent painful events, she could find a different kind of peace—not perfect, but real.

As the sky grew dark, exhaustion settled in. She slipped under the quilt in her bedroom, her body sinking into the comfortable mattress, and listened to the unfamiliar sounds of her new home. Tomorrow would bring its own battles with doubt, but for now, the little blue cottage offered shelter from both the past and the future.

# Chapter 2

"Good morning, Reinvention Day." *I might as well try to start with a positive vibe.*

Tammy threw off the covers, swung her legs over the side of the bed, and padded across to the window. The rising sun painted the town in shades of orange and pink, beckoning her to explore.

She tucked her feet into a pair of slippers and made her way to the kitchen, brewing a steaming cup of coffee. As she stepped out onto the porch, she inhaled deeply, the crisp morning air filling her lungs. The dew-kissed grass glistened in the early light, inviting her into the garden.

Tammy set her mug on the railing and ventured into the lush greenery. Her fingers trailed along delicate petals and rough leaves as she wandered through the beds. Vibrant colors caught her eye—sunny yellow, deep purple, and soft pink. The sweet scent of lavender wafted from the side fence.

She paused at a cluster of creamy white flowers with tiny star-shaped blooms. Elderflower. Tammy recognized it from her research for one of her novels. Her expertise with plants centered around their lethal properties, but that didn't stop her from admiring their beauty. She bent over, breathing in their subtle, honey-like fragrance. The garden was in full bloom, despite the cottage being empty for some time.

As she continued her exploration, several plants lay snapped in half. Delicate petals were strewn across the soil. She knelt, inspecting the damaged flora. *What happened here?*

Tammy bit her lip. The broken stems and wilted leaves seemed to mock her incompetence. Her fingers twitched to do something, but these were living things requiring care she didn't know how to give. She was unprepared for this responsibility and feared she'd only make it worse.

She stood, brushing dirt from her knees. Something had been through here—perhaps a rabbit or a gusty wind? Her mystery writer's mind wanted answers, but her gardener's inexperience demanded help. Tammy made a mental note to seek advice. Wasn't that why she moved to Willowcroft—for new experiences and to let new people in?

The last sip of coffee had gone cold. She stepped back inside to prepare for the day. She had a town to explore.

Her sandals clicked against the sidewalk as she ambled toward the square. The morning sun caught the store's striped awnings—crisp white paired with cherry red, ocean blue, and tangerine orange—creating a carnival-like canopy.

It was like walking into a Hallmark Christmas movie, minus the snow. Unlike LA's steel and glass, the century-old brick buildings wore their age like a badge of honor, their weathered cornices telling stories of decades past. A shopkeeper chatted with a mailman, both seemingly content to let time flow at its own pace.

Remnants of streamers and deflated balloons hung around the lampposts. Had she just missed a town event like a pie contest or a harvest festival? The kind of small-town events that filled cozy mysteries—the genre she was considering for revitalizing her writing career. Thriller mysteries were too stressful right now.

The town hall clock chimed the quarter hour. Two women paused their conversation to check the time—not by pulling out their smartphones, but by glancing up at the tower itself, just as generations before them must have done. In LA, she moved fast, always ready for a meeting or deadline. Here even the pigeons' struts were slower across the cobblestones, unworried about being shooed away.

Spices and buttery pastry curled through the air, drawing a growl from her stomach. She followed the scent to the Sweet Crumbs bakery, its sunny yellow-and-white awning glowing beside the cool green-and-white stripes of the bookstore next door.

Inside, a round, jolly woman greeted Tammy.

"Good morning, lovely!" the woman said as her rosy cheeks dimpled. "I'm Mrs. Applewood. Welcome to our blissful bakery!"

Tammy returned the infectious energy with a cheesy grin.

"How are you settling in at the little blue cottage?" the woman asked.

"How did you know?"

"We've been expecting you. I helped make the sign on your door. I do hope it was still there when you arrived."

"Yes, it was, and such a thoughtful touch. Thank you." Tammy extended her hand across the counter. "I'm Tammy Rumbelow."

Mrs. Applewood waved it off and came around. "That won't do, my lovely. You're one of us now."

Before Tammy could react, two arms encircled her. Her body tensed, old defenses snapping into place. But as the seconds ticked by, something in the hug felt different—no hidden agenda, no expectations. Like the damaged plants in her garden, Tammy's barriers needed tending. Did healing start by accepting help? She leaned in, her rigid posture softening despite the alarms blaring in her mind.

Tammy blinked back tears.

"There now. You've been officially welcomed to town." Mrs. Applewood released Tammy and returned behind the counter as if the experience was an everyday occurrence. "That cottage has been empty for too long."

Tammy took a deep breath.

"Now, what can I get for you this fine morning? The cinnamon rolls are straight out of the oven."

Was this how people treated each other here? In LA, people rushed by, eyes glued to their phones. Trust and real relationships were rare commodities. But Mrs. Applewood seemed genuine. An unfamiliar emotion, yes, but that was the point of her second chance—learning to recognize authenticity when it appeared.

Her stomach filled with pastries and her mind wrestling with possibility, she left the bakery. The cynic in her waited for the other shoe to drop, but a newer, braver part of her wondered if Willowcroft might be different.

The bell above the door chimed melodiously as Tammy entered the bookstore she'd seen upon arriving in town. The bay window under the green-and-white awning let in the morning sun, which highlighted a wonderful display and a carousel of shiny brochures. The scent of new print mixed with aged pages filled the air as she took in the multiple rows of bookshelves. *There is nothing better than escaping into a book.*

"Hello!" a cheerful voice called out from behind the counter. Tammy turned to see a woman with short, wavy auburn hair framed by black-rimmed glasses perched on her nose. Her hazel eyes beamed with curiosity, beckoning conversation.

"Hi, I'm Tammy," she replied, stepping closer. The woman's top lip sucked in the bottom one as if stifling a smile. *Was she stopping herself from saying something? Does she know I bought the cottage too?*

"Welcome to Bookworm Haven! I'm Olivia, the owner."

"I love the name."

"Thank you. When I was a kid, my sister teased me, calling me a bookworm like it was something to be ashamed of."

Tammy recollected the taunts she'd received from supposed friends and reviewers alike. "I think loving books is a wonderful thing."

Olivia laughed. "I agree. That's why I turned it into something positive. Willowcroft became my haven of acceptance, so I named the bookstore Bookworm Haven. It's a safe place for all book lovers, where being a bookworm is celebrated."

"That's beautiful. How long have you had the store?"

"Fifteen years now. Instead of throwing me a twenty-first birthday party, my father gave me the money to buy this place and my apartment upstairs."

"Wow, that's quite a gift!" *What did I get for my twenty-first? Can't have been anything special if I don't even remember.*

"Yes, it was. My older sister had a lavish event in Manhattan. For the same cost, I got a home and a lifelong business here in Willowcroft."

*I'd choose a bookstore over a party too.* "Well, it's amazing and oozes love and history," Tammy said, glancing around the cozy atmosphere.

"It's my little piece of paradise, and I'm glad to share it with fellow book lovers. Plus, in the summer, it's quite the hub for visitors."

"How so?"

"Without a tourist information center in town, my store fills the role. We get tourists wanting state park trail maps and brochures about the local wildlife, like bears." Olivia gestured to the brochure carousel in the window. "Those pamphlets bring them in, and some stay to browse and buy books on birdwatching, survival skills, and so on."

"Brilliant. You've created a community hub, resource center, and an up-sell all in one." *She's one shrewd businesswoman.*

Olivia's eyes sparkled. "Having the park entrance off the square is great for the town and my store. It keeps the place lively, and I get to meet so many interesting people, like you."

"I'm sure I'll be spending a lot of time here." *It's a perfect venue for a book launch.*

"You're always welcome. Now do tell, what brings you to Willowcroft?"

*What am I supposed to say? The two people I trusted the most destroyed me? That I'm running because otherwise I'd drown?* Tammy glanced at the books on a display table, hoping the titles might offer her a way out. "Oh, you know...just needed a change of scenery."

Olivia's gaze lingered, as if she knew there was more. Tammy quickly added, "I've always wanted to live in a small town."

Not a lie, but it wasn't the truth either.

Tammy browsed the shelves, their rows brimming with everything from mysteries to romance. The bookshelves and their owner were magnetic and warm, filled with hidden gems waiting to be discovered.

"Wow, you have quite the collection of mystery novels," Tammy called out from the stacks, picking up a well-worn copy from her *Deception Chronicles* series.

"Yes, I've always been drawn to the mysterious and unexplained. There's something thrilling about delving into the unknown and solving puzzles, don't you think?"

"Absolutely." Tammy's delight grew with each shared sentiment. "Mysteries have always fascinated me."

"A kindred spirit! I can't resist untangling cryptic clues."

"I love getting pulled into a dramatic plot and figuring out 'whodunit' before the detective does."

"Me too!" Olivia laughed. "I have a side hustle as a genealogist. People's family histories are big mysteries needing unraveling."

"I'd never thought of genealogy like that. But I'm hooked." Tammy returned to the counter having chosen four books. "I'm so glad I found your store today."

"So am I."

Tammy leaned in. *Do I have two friends in Willowcroft already? It wasn't so hard.* "Thank you for inviting me into your world of mysteries. I can't wait for an adventure together."

"So...are you working on your next novel?" Olivia asked.

"How did you know I was a writer?" *It's going to be an adjustment getting used to everyone knowing everything about me.*

"Oh, word gets around in a small town like this. I'd heard a mystery writer named Tammy had bought the little blue cottage, and we don't get many newcomers. Besides, you aren't wearing hiking boots and have a creative spark in your eye."

Tammy laughed. "Yes, I'm Tammy Rumbelow. You have most of my books."

"I've read your whole series. I can't wait to read the next installment set in our quaint little town."

Tammy grinned. "I'm thinking of branching out into cozy mysteries." She looked out the bay window. "Willowcroft qualifies as a quintessential setting for one, don't you think?"

Olivia rang up Tammy's purchases, a guide to flower gardens, a local history book, and two cozies for research purposes.

With a wave, she stepped out of the bookstore into the main square.

The woman stood like a colorful statue amid the bustle of the town square where children laughed and played around the unusual water fountain. She had an air of eccentricity with her gray hair tied in a neat bun, and draped in a deep red shawl resembling a ripe cherry almost bordering on burgundy. Her eyes, sharp and observant. A strange pull drew Tammy toward the enigmatic figure.

"Hello, dear," the woman said. "I've been hoping to run into you."

"Oh?"

The woman's gaze never wavered from her. "You're our newest resident—in the little blue cottage, aren't you?"

*Was it announced in the newspaper or something?* It had taken two years to meet the tenant in the apartment next to hers in LA. And this woman would make three people in a few hours. "Yes, I moved in yesterday."

"I've lived here for over seventy years, all my life. Not much happens without me hearing about it. My Harold was the town doctor, and I taught history at the high school."

This was the reality of small-town life living up to the cliché of everyone knowing everything. "Well, it's very nice to meet you..."

"Mrs. Temperance."

"Mrs. Temperance, I'm Tammy Rumbelow. Recent arrival from Los Angeles."

"Welcome to Willowcroft! I helped Mrs. Applewood and Olivia with the sign on your door."

*Was it a town event?*

"What made you leave Los Angeles?"

Tammy gripped the strap of her bag. *Why didn't I prepare an answer to this question?* "Ah...well...I got tired of the smog and noise and such."

Mrs. Temperance squinted. "Whatever the reason—"

*She knows there's more.*

"—I hope you'll find our little town to your liking. It must seem quite different from the big city. But I think you'll discover we have our own charm."

The twinkle in Mrs. Temperance's eyes intrigued Tammy. "You have stories."

"You're perceptive, my dear. I do have my fair share of tales."

"Would you mind sharing some of them with me?" She was eager to learn anything and everything about Willowcroft.

"Perhaps." A mysterious expression crossed her face. "But first, let's get to know each other. There's much to be shared between friends, after all."

Mrs. Temperance linked her arm with Tammy's. "You've noticed our fountain."

Tammy had never seen a design like it. "It's unique."

"Indeed. It doubles as a war memorial. A living tribute to the fallen."

"That's a lovely sentiment."

"It's been the centerpiece of our square for a hundred years." Mrs. Temperance gestured at the ground. "Along with these nineteenth-century stones."

Tammy looked to her feet. "I never expected to see cobblestones in Michigan. They're charming."

"They are rare in these parts, and nearly lost in the eighties when the council wanted to asphalt everything." Mrs. Temperance's chin lifted and her silver bun sparkled in the sun. "My friend Marjorie and I staged sit-ins and more to save them."

"Well done."

The older woman's eyes clouded over with what Tammy sensed as pride.

"Sometimes preservation requires a touch of rebellion," said Mrs. Temperance.

As they spoke, movement flickered in the corner of Tammy's eye. A black-and-white cat slunk across the street. It moved with stealthy grace, stopping to sniff at something.

"How cute," Tammy remarked, watching its plumed tail sway back and forth. "Is it yours, Mrs. Temperance?"

"No! You've spotted our resident stray. He, too, is a recent arrival. He helped the sheriff catch a prankster only a couple of days ago. Bit of a town celebrity since then."

Tammy appraised the feline, noting the uncanny intelligence in its eyes. They gleamed with curiosity, almost as if they were assessing her, like quiet observers with secrets of their own.

While driving cross-country, she had imagined getting a pet to curl up with, a companion to share her adventures. Someone to talk to, even if the conversation was one-sided. Was the universe bringing two strays together? If he truly needed a home, why not hers? They could settle into Willowcroft as a pair, though it sounded like he had already wormed his way into the heart of the town.

Tammy approached slowly, hoping not to frighten him away. As she drew nearer, she reached into her purse and pulled out a small packet of crackers she had packed earlier.

"Here, kitty." She crumbled the crackers. "Are you hungry?"

The cat observed her, its green eyes never leaving her face. It moved forward, sniffing at the food before taking a sample.

"See? I won't hurt you." Tammy needed a safe connection without an ulterior motive. This furry creature, with its own issues to overcome, might be her first step toward opening herself up again.

"You have a good heart, dear," Mrs. Temperance said.

As the cat finished the last crumb, it looked at Tammy, its green eyes held a depth of understanding. At that moment, they bonded.

"How about..." *I need to think about this.* "Pawlock Holmes?" Tammy asked, rolling the name over her tongue as she studied the black-and-white fur on the cat's face. "Would you like to live with me?"

The cat paused as if considering her offer, its eyes narrowing before it took another step toward Tammy, a silent acceptance of her invitation. He needed her—and she needed him.

"Do you like the name? We can call you Lockie for short." The newly named Lockie blinked at her and let out a rusty purr. "Let's get you settled at home." Tammy scooped the cat into her arms and held him close. "And some real food."

Tammy needed supplies for herself and Lockie. "Mrs. Temperance, where can I get groceries and pet supplies around town?"

"Stonefield by the highway, has a plaza with all the usual big names. But if you're looking for something local," she gestured across the square, "Mrs. Hubbard's Cupboard with the purple and white awning is the place to go. It's our general store where you can find groceries, household items, and even pet products for your new furry friend. Marjorie used to run it. Now it's her daughter-in-law Katie's store, as it was Marjorie's mother-in-law's before her."

"Wow, multiple generations of women running the business. I'll check it out."

"We may not have it all in Willowcroft, but across the five towns forming *Greater* Willowcroft, every convenience you might need is available. There's even a free community bus linking us all."

"I'm so glad I met you, Mrs. Temperance. You are a wealth of knowledge. I hope this is the start of a wonderful friendship."

On returning to the little blue cottage, supplies in hand, Lockie leaped from Tammy's arms to explore his new surroundings, sniffing and examining every corner and crevice. She watched with amusement as the cat claimed the space, feeling a growing connection.

Tammy gave a contented sigh as she sank into the cozy armchair by the fireplace. What a whirlwind first full day in Willowcroft.

Despite her initial reservations about moving to such a small, quiet town, the warmth and kindness she had experienced so far from Olivia, Mrs. Temperance, and Mrs. Applewood had put her at ease. After years in bustling Los Angeles, the slower pace and neighborly atmosphere was a refreshing change.

Still, a nagging apprehension lingered. Recent events—and her mother—had made her cautious and cynical. She was now quick to question the intentions behind even the kindest gestures.

As Lockie nestled on her lap, Tammy stroked his soft fur. Meeting Olivia and browsing at her charming bookstore proved delightful. She wanted to believe Olivia's bookish enthusiasm, Mrs. Temperance's matronly concern, and Mrs. Applewood's warm welcome were genuine. But were they? Did the townspeople have their own agenda for embracing her arrival?

Tammy glanced down at her cat. "What do you think, boy? Can I trust them?"

Lockie seemed to sense her inner turmoil. He stood and stretched before head-butting her chin. She appreciated the affectionate gesture. A scratch behind his ears elicited a deep, rumbling purr.

He circled her lap and made biscuits on her thighs, claiming Tammy as his own. The rhythmic motion and heat from his body calmed her nerves for a moment.

*Who can I trust?* Her mother's voice entered her head, "You're too naive. People will only use you."

Memories of LA surged forward—the people closest to her proved her mom's warnings. Why had she come to Willowcroft? To escape them.

*Maybe Mom was right.* A suffocating thought. But then she remembered Mrs. Applewood's hug and Olivia's smile—they didn't feel calculated.

"No, I have to give them a chance. I need to follow my instincts and believe I can find true friends here. This is my opportunity to prove to myself, and to my mother, that trust doesn't have to be a mistake."

She looked at Lockie. "You like it here, don't you?" The cat gazed at her, blinking slowly as if in agreement. "You're a wise one, aren't you?" Tammy scratched under his chin. He leaned into her touch. "Well, if you think I can give them the benefit of the doubt, I guess I will until proven otherwise."

For now, she would remain open, yet cautious.

# Chapter 3

Lockie's weight pressed against Tammy's feet. "Good morning, you."

The cat lifted his head and offered a slow blink, already making himself at home after just one night.

She swung her legs out of bed and padded to the window, tugging the blind upward. Sunlight flooded the room, forcing her to squint. As her vision cleared, movement caught her eye.

A figure sprinted past her swinging gate, scattering leaves and petals in their wake like some twisted version of a flower girl. The bizarre trail marked his path along the empty street. His dark, unkempt hair stuck out at odd angles, matching the wild scruff of his beard. Despite the summer morning heat, he wore a heavy winter coat, its tails flapping behind him like broken wings.

What in the world?

"He's got to be roasting." Lockie joined her at the window, his tail swishing in a steady rhythm as the peculiar scene unfolded.

She pressed closer to the glass. The man glanced back, his eyes wide and darting, searching as if expecting pursuit. His clenched jaw and grinding teeth were visible even from a distance.

Who was he? And why was he running?

"Hello, Willowcroft." *I guess it's living up to the quirky small-town cliché.*

Lockie seemed equally perplexed by the spectacle.

Tammy shrugged her shoulders and went about her morning routine, with her feline companion close behind. He wound around her legs, meowing, as she prepared breakfast. "Okay, I'll get you some food too," she laughed, filling a bowl. The cat pounced on it, scarfing it down.

"Whoa there, tiger. No one's going to steal it from you."

She marveled at how it had only been a day, but already this furball had wormed his way into her heart. In this town, with its apparent oddities, it was comforting to have a friend by her side.

"Well," she said after eating, "how about we have a relaxing morning?"

Tammy sank into the plush couch and opened one of the cozy mysteries she'd bought from Olivia's bookstore. Lockie leaped onto her lap, kneading her thighs before curling into a tight ball. The gentle rumble of his purr vibrated against her skin.

"You're making it difficult to focus on the story." She scratched behind his ears. Lockie's eyes slid shut in contentment.

She turned the page, enjoying the serenity enveloping her cottage. No blaring horns, no shouting neighbors—just the musical birdsong outside her window and steady cat purrs.

"I could get used to this."

Lockie sprang from Tammy's lap, landing with a soft thud on a nearby cardboard box.

"I should probably unpack those soon, huh?" She placed a bookmark in her book and stared at the rows of boxes. "Or...I mean, I don't need every single thing out and displayed right now, right?"

There was a comfort in keeping things half packed, like she hadn't quite committed to this opportunity yet.

Her gaze drifted upward. "The online listing mentioned an attic. I wonder if it's suitable for storage?"

Lockie meowed, as if in agreement.

"Want to explore with me, buddy?" She set her book aside and stood, stretching her arms above her head. "Might as well check it out."

Tammy made her way to a door off the corridor. Lockie bounded ahead, arriving before her, his tail high as he waited.

The brass knob was cool against her palm as she turned it, revealing steep, wooden stairs. What relics might be stowed away?

Lockie bounded up two stairs at a time.

"Wait up!" At the first step, a guttural creak. "Okay, lesson learned. Tread lightly."

She grasped the railing and ascended with careful steps. The groaning wood reverberated around the narrow stairwell.

"In thriller novels, this is when something jumps out and—"

"Meow!"

Tammy startled and tightened her grip on the handrail to steady herself. "Lockie! You scared the wits out of me."

The stairs opened into a dim cavern of sloped ceilings and exposed wooden beams. Muted light entered through the small windows at each end.

"This is...atmospheric."

She tiptoed forward, wary of loose flooring. Dust motes swirled in the pale shafts of sunlight, making her cough. "Hmm, needs cleaning. But plenty of room for boxes, right?"

Her feline companion offered no response, having disappeared into the shadows.

Tammy's writer's imagination kicked into overdrive. "Perfect setting for a ghost story..."

A soft, scuttling sound stole her attention.

"Lockie?" she whispered. "That better be you and not some attic-dwelling creature." Her eyes darted around the shadowy space.

Gathering courage, she slunk toward the back corner, brushing cobwebs aside. "If this were one of my novels, there'd be a skeleton back here, or at least a—" Her words stuck in her throat as something caught her eye—a yellowed paper peeked out from beneath a warped floorboard. Curiosity overrode any fear as she eased it from its hiding place. Dust billowed, tickling her nose and making her eyes water. She didn't care. She was too captivated by what she held—an aged envelope, its edges frayed and color weathered by time.

"Hello, what is this?" She searched for her feline companion. "Lockie! Come look. We've stumbled into one of my mystery novels!"

The cat darted out of the shadows and sniffed at the fragile find. Tammy swept away years of accumulated grime, the resulting cloud causing Lockie to sneeze.

"It's been here for ages." Was it a love letter? A confession? Her writer's mind crafted multiple narratives.

She turned it over. The faded writing gave the cottage's address. A smudged postmark sat in the corner. She ran her finger along the seal, hesitating.

A knot of anxiety twisted in her stomach, a voice in her head urging her to leave it be—to close the attic door, and forget this ever happened. But the writer in her, who thrived on creating mysteries, wouldn't let go. What if this was the key to some long-forgotten secret? The kind that might change everything.

"Should we take a peek?"

Lockie nudged Tammy's hand with his nose. Did he agree?

She couldn't walk away from this. Whoever hid this letter considered it important enough to conceal it in the floorboards of an attic. Her curiosity overpowered her nerves.

With careful precision, her trembling fingers pried the flap loose. Inside, a single sheet of paper crackled as she unfolded it. Time had erased most of the writing, sparing one solitary section. Her eyes locked on the remaining words.

"If anyone finds out, you'll get it. You'd better leave town or else."

Tammy's breath hitched. The years hadn't dulled the threat's sharp edge. Who had written this? And to whom? She swallowed hard, the implications unfurling. Was this a promise? Or a desperate plea? Either way, someone who had lived in this very house had been in danger. Goosebumps erupted across her body.

She re-read it.

"What secret was worth threatening a life over?" The curious writer in her needed to uncover the truth behind the warning. "We can't ignore this."

Lockie meowed, rubbing against her leg. Tammy stroked his fur, her eyes fixated on the letter.

"This is... this is serious. Someone in Willowcroft was hiding something big."

The thought gnawed at her. Trusting the wrong people left marks. Secrets and lies scarred everything they touched. A part of her screamed to toss the letter aside. This was exactly the kind of mystery she'd spent years crafting in her books—a secret hidden for decades, threatening to unravel. But it always led to a death. Curiosity warred with caution. She'd come to Willowcroft for peace, not danger. But she had to know. She couldn't just walk away.

A sharp creak downstairs pulled her attention. "Did you hear that?" she whispered to Lockie, who had already arched his back, fur bristling.

Could someone be looking for the letter? Or was it her imagination?

A louder noise followed—a sharp scrape of metal on metal. Her heart leaped into her throat. That was real.

The sound repeated. Was the front door being forced?

She tucked the letter into her pocket as she crept toward the stairwell.

Panic swirled in her chest, fighting with the instinct to stay put, to lock herself in the attic and wait for it to pass. But something stronger—maybe stupidity, or the same curiosity that had her fingers itching to open the envelope—urged her forward. But did she want to face whatever—or whoever—it was?

Forcing a deep inhale, she started down the creaking stairs, cringing at every groan.

"Hello?... Is someone there?"

Silence.

Time slowed with each step. The old wood protested under her feet. Lockie remained at her heels. She paused at the bottom, straining her ears for any sign of an intruder. The house seemed to hold its breath.

Gathering her courage, she rounded the corner to the entryway. The front door stood locked. Tammy's hand quivered as she double-checked the deadbolt.

She pressed her eye to the peephole, scanning the porch and yard. The gate had closed. Was that the noise she heard? She chewed her lower lip.

"What do you think? Should we check it out?"

Lockie meowed and flicked his tail.

She steeled herself. "Okay, buddy."

She scooped up the cat, holding him like a furry shield. Her fingers shook as she grasped the doorknob.

"Sorry about this, but if anyone's out there, you might need to channel your inner tiger."

Taking a deep breath, Tammy yanked the door open, thrusting Lockie through the air. "Who's there?" her voice cracked.

The porch stood empty. Nearby shrubs swayed.

Lockie squirmed in her arms, clearly unimpressed with his role as a feline bodyguard.

Tammy's shoulders lowered. She set him down, crouching to scratch behind his ears. "I'm so sorry, buddy. That wasn't fair of me, was it? I panicked."

She stepped outside. A flash of movement caught her eye—a fleeting human shadow at the far end of the lane.

"Hey!" Tammy shouted, but the stranger had already crested the hill, continuing further out of town.

It wasn't the same man as before. No winter coat, no wild hair—this one was younger, dressed in cargo shorts and a blue T-shirt, moving with startling speed. As he darted away, she glimpsed a yellow circle on his shirt—perhaps a logo or some kind of graphic. It was familiar, but he was too quick for her to be sure.

"Did you see that?" The cat's tail twitched back and forth, his eyes fixed on the spot where the figure had vanished.

Who was he? Had he lurked outside her door? Two men running—both acting like they were escaping something. Were they connected? These incidents surpassed anything she experienced in LA.

Tammy's chest pulsed as she closed and locked the door. She leaned against it, taking deep breaths to calm herself. "What have I stumbled into, Lockie?"

The cat meowed, rubbing her ankles.

Her legs weak, she sagged to the floor.

"First that weird guy this morning, the creepy letter, now this..."

She pulled out the envelope. "Does this secret still matter to someone?"

A shiver coursed through her as the implications sank in. "Some new beginning this turned out to be, huh?"

Was Willowcroft's charming veneer masking secrets?

"I came here to start over. Not to stumble into some small-town conspiracy."

"Meow."

She sighed, her fingers drumming the floorboards. "But I can't ignore this, can I?"

*Maybe I'll get a novel out of it.*

Tammy's jaw set, determination replacing any lingering fear. "If I'm going to make a home here, I need the truth. About the town, about its people." *And my house.*

She scrambled to her feet, startling Lockie. "What do you think, partner? Ready to play detective?"

The cat arched its back, then scratched at the door.

Tammy chuckled. "I'll take that as a yes."

Her fingers traced the edge of the letter. Should she show Olivia? She seemed genuine—nothing like her ex-best friend, Sally, with her sugar-sweet encouragement and razor-sharp betrayal. Still, they had once been genuine.

Lockie let out a single meow and butted his head against her leg.

She was in Willowcroft for a fresh start, not to wallow in past hurts. And sometimes the only way to learn to trust again was to risk being wrong.

She grabbed her keys. "Let's go to Bookworm Haven."

# Chapter 4

Tammy burst into the bookstore, the bell above the door clattering. Lockie darted in behind her, almost tripping her in his haste. She caught sight of Olivia and Mrs. Temperance huddled by the counter, their conversation dying midsentence. She ignored their startled expressions as she thrust the envelope forward.

"You won't believe what I found in the attic!"

"Tammy, dear, what is it?" asked Mrs. Temperance.

For a moment, she hesitated, her fingers inching toward her pocket. Were they trustworthy? What if they dismissed her or—worse—used her story as gossip? Olivia's kind expression nudged her resolve. *My first test. And I'm going to ace it.* She passed it over.

Olivia opened the envelope and read it aloud. She looked at Tammy with wide eyes.

"How extraordinary." She handed it to Mrs. Temperance, who scrutinized it, lips pursed.

"Well, I never..." She met Tammy's gaze. "This raises some troubling questions."

"Right." Tammy slumped against the counter. "It's so mysterious. It threatened someone living in my cottage. We have to find out who they were and why they did it."

Mrs. Temperance ran her fingers along the letter's edges. "This is quite intriguing. Willowcroft has its fair share of secrets, but this..." She paused, tapping her chin. "I can't imagine what it refers to."

"Then we must investigate!" said Olivia. "If something sinister happened here in the past, we need to uncover it. This is our next mystery to solve, Mrs. Temperance!"

"It certainly is."

Tammy's heart skipped for joy at the prospect of joining forces to unravel the mystery. "What do you mean by your *next* mystery?"

Olivia glanced at the older woman with a big grin. "We solved a mystery last week. Willowcroft's Great Bear Caper! We had three bear visits, including one on Mrs. Temperance's porch and one that broke through my store's window."

Tammy gasped. "Are we safe in town? I didn't factor bears into my plan."

"Don't worry, dear," Mrs. Temperance reassured her. "In all my seventy-plus years, we've never had bear trouble—until last week. But black bears are harmless."

*Phew.* "How did you solve the mystery?"

"Well," said Olivia, "Mrs. Temperance, with her knowledge of honey terroir, traced the honey back to the Bradley Berry Farm store. I caught *Nick* Bradley on my CCTV and he confessed to luring the bears with honey and berries." She pulled a newspaper from under the counter. "You can read about it here."

Tammy looked at the front-page headline: "The Great Willowcroft Bear Caper" and the paper's date. "This happened just before I arrived!"

"Yes. And it sparked our desire to solve more mysteries," Mrs. Temperance said, turning to Olivia, who nodded in agreement.

"Wow. I thought my week was adventurous with a night at a haunted hotel," Tammy said. "But bears? You win."

Olivia's eyes lit up. "Haunted hotel? Oh, do tell!"

"I will, but not right now. All I can think about is this letter...and now bears." She grimaced.

"Fair enough," Olivia said. "What should we investigate first?"

The cryptic words eclipsed the idea of bear visits. Who wrote it? And the recipient—did they flee, or stand their ground?

"My bookstore houses an extensive collection of local history books. I'll comb through those for hints."

*We're really doing this.* An investigation. A chance to peel back the layers of Willowcroft and its inhabitants. *That's one way to get to know people.* Her writer's instincts tingled. "I'll scour the newspaper archives at the library and dig into the cottage's past residents."

"Great ideas," Mrs. Temperance said. "I'll bring it up at the knitting circle meeting. If anyone knows anything, it will be one of them." She looked at her watch. "Speaking of the Willow-Crafters, I need to get home so they aren't knocking on my door in the middle of baking!"

"It's settled," Olivia declared. "We're investigating."

"Let's meet back here tomorrow evening to share what we've learned," Tammy suggested.

The two women agreed without hesitation.

Mrs. Temperance rushed out the door. "Must dash, my dears."

*She's sprightly for her age.*

Tammy bid her own farewell and walked home with Lockie, her imagination a swirl of questions. Who had lived in the cottage before her? What sinister events prompted such a chilling letter? The ominous warning haunted her thoughts. "If anyone finds out, you'll get it. You'd better leave town or else." She shuddered, the hair on her arms prickling. What had the author known that others didn't? Would they really kill over it?

A mystery to solve at her own house gave Tammy a renewed sense of purpose. *With Olivia's research skills and Mrs. Temperance's connections, I'm sure we'll uncover new information.*

Mrs. Hazel Temperance hurried home. The letter flashed into her thoughts. But there was no time to ruminate on it now. She had just enough time to bake the tart she'd prepped earlier before the doorbell rang.

"Hazel!" Marjorie greeted her with a hug as she stepped inside. "Something smells divine."

"Apple nutmeg tart. Fresh from the oven."

"Oh, how lovely!" Betty said, following close behind. "You do spoil us."

One by one, the ladies of the Willowcroft knitting circle arrived. Known as the Willow-Crafters, they settled in for an afternoon of knitting, eating, laughing, and gossiping. The clicking of needles mingled with the clink of teacups and friendly chatter. Marjorie was working on a soft blue button-up sweater for her newest grandchild, while Betty was getting an early start on a cabled Christmas scarf. Mrs. Beatrice Smith wrangled with her slip stitch.

"I met the new owner of the little blue cottage," Hazel mentioned casually, reaching for a slice of tart. "Her name is Tammy Rumbelow, a mystery writer from Los Angeles."

"How exciting!" said Betty. "I've been dying to meet her. What's she like?"

"She's a lovely young woman. She's adopted the black-and-white stray cat that's been hanging around town."

Marjorie paused her needles. "Is that so? I trust she won't bring any shenanigans with her from the city."

"Oh, I hope she does. That would be so much fun," said Betty.

"I'm not sensing any tomfoolery from her. I don't believe there's any cause for concern," Hazel said. "Tammy seems quite taken with the cottage, though. She's interested in learning more about its history."

"History of the little blue cottage?" Marjorie asked.

"Yes. She found an old letter hidden in the attic, and it's got us all intrigued."

Betty set down her knitting. "What sort of letter?"

"Well," Hazel hesitated, remembering her promise to be discreet. "Let's just say it has Tammy curious about the previous tenants."

"It's had a patchy rental history as far back as I can remember," said Marjorie.

"I can't recall any specific stories about the house or its tenants. Does anyone remember any rumors featuring the cottage?" Hazel asked, trying to sound casual as she continued knitting.

"I'm sure every building in this town has skeletons in their closets, but nothing comes to mind," said Betty as she flopped back into the chair.

"Was there something about a love affair?" Beatrice offered with a wrinkled forehead.

That got Betty's attention as she sat forward. "A secret love affair? How romantic..."

Hazel caught Marjorie rolling her eyes in Betty's direction. Her two friends couldn't be more different from each other if one were a hydrangea and the other an oak tree. But she loved them both for their own individual qualities.

Hazel filed away the affair story, but without more to go on, she wasn't certain it would be useful. *I hope the others are having more luck.* "It's strange how some places hold their secrets so tightly. But perhaps that's what makes them all the more intriguing."

Betty leaned in. "Well, if there is something to be uncovered, I'm sure you'll get to the bottom of it, Hazel." Her animation increased. "Maybe Tammy will write a book about it!"

Marjorie clucked her tongue and paused her knitting needles for a moment. "She'd better not use us as characters. I'm not ready for my close-up!"

The group erupted into laughter, their chuckles filling the room. With the mystery discussion reaching a natural pause, Hazel shifted the conversation back to lighter fare. "Now, speaking of town tales, Marjorie, do share what you've heard recently."

"I'm not one for gossip..."

It was Betty's turn to roll her eyes at Marjorie.

Hazel bit back a smile. Marjorie's penchant for gossip was well known, but she'd deny it to her grave.

"You won't believe the latest from Mrs. Hubbard's Cupboard," she said, dropping to a whisper.

Marjorie's daughter-in-law, Katie, did an excellent job of keeping the store's reputation as a local gossip hub intact.

"Just yesterday..."

Tammy glanced at the letter again, its chilling words standing out against the aged paper. "If anyone finds out, you'll get it. You'd better leave town or else." The threat was real, and it was here, in her new haven. The charm of Willowcroft was now tainted with a sense of danger. Was her fresh start doomed?

She thought about the people she'd met. Could she trust them? Her stomach churned at the thought of betrayal. Her mother's voice taunted her, "You're making the same mistakes."

She pictured Mrs. Applewood and Olivia. *I have to give them a chance.* This was her opportunity to begin again, to prove to herself, and her mom, she was capable of this.

The stakes extended beyond emotional well-being. Ignoring it might be risky, but pursuing it risked shattering her perception of Willowcroft—a town she hoped to call home.

The rising moon caught her eye. Would danger follow the letter? What if discovering the truth behind the words was the path to starting over?

# Chapter 5

Tammy stepped onto the porch. The crisp morning breeze whisked away the remnants of last night's doubt. The sunrise reminded her of the watercolor paintings in her editor's office—the kind of peaceful scene she'd always wanted to write about but never quite managed between her darker plotlines.

The sweet scent of blooming flowers surrounded her, a far cry from the gasoline-tinged smog she'd left behind. The dew on the field sparkled like tiny gemstones, and the birds—not helicopters or sirens—serenaded her from the treetops. *So, this is what mornings are supposed to feel like.*

As she locked the door, Lockie darted past her legs. He sniffed every blade of grass and flower petal. She followed the cat, intending to admire her garden before heading to the library.

Her joy faltered at a startling sight. The flowerbed along the front fence looked...wrong. The lush array of blooms now contained a conspicuous hole.

What on earth? Tammy crouched to examine the damage. Several flowerbeds had been disturbed, roots and all. Clumps of dirt lay scattered around, and deep furrows marred the soil. *This feels like the setup to a mystery novel*—The Puzzle of the Pilfered Plants.

Had someone ransacked her garden? An absurd thought, yet here was the evidence. She recalled the man scurrying away from her property the previous morning. *Was he the culprit, or am I letting my imagination run wild again?* Her mother interrupted, *not everything is a story waiting to happen.* She shook off the thought.

"What do you make of this, Lockie?"

The cat sniffed at the disturbed earth before pawing at Tammy's leg, urging her toward the gate.

"You're right. We have a bigger mystery to solve at the library. And this... Maybe it's kids playing a prank on the new person?"

Whatever it was, the bizarre incident would have to wait. She stood, brushing dirt from her hands and knees. As they made their way down the path, Tammy cast one last troubled glance at her ravaged flowerbed. There was no denying the missing plants nagged at her, but one puzzle at a time.

Pushing it out of her mind, Tammy and Lockie bounded along the sidewalk with the sun on her face growing warmer. The local library awaited—*my personal gold mine of forgotten tales*—across the square from Olivia's bookstore.

She stepped off the sidewalk and pushed open the heavy wooden doors of the old brick building. The scent of aging paper and rich leather enveloped her, a comforting embrace inviting her in. Tammy scanned the main room, taking in the towering shelves packed tight with stories. Golden beams of light shone through arched windows, illuminating swirling motes of dust. Memories flooded back to childhood afternoons spent exploring hidden corners of libraries, each discovery transporting her to other worlds. She inhaled, savoring the familiar aroma. Beside her, Lockie twitched his whiskers; she assumed he shared her enthusiasm. "Smells like adventure, doesn't it?" she whispered to him.

Her gaze shifted to the librarian's severe expression and half-moon glasses perched on her nose, which made Tammy pause. *Why do they all look like they stepped out of central casting for "Strict Librarian #1"?* But she'd learned appearances could be deceiving. Some of the sternest-looking librarians were as soft inside as a well-worn paperback inside. *Let's hope this one's more romance bestseller than dusty encyclopedia.*

Tammy cleared her throat to catch the attention of the bespectacled woman engrossed in a thick volume. Lockie meowed, offering his own form of introduction. A flush crept up her neck. *Shh! Don't let her hear you.*

"Excuse me. I was wondering if you had any information about the little blue cottage on Cedar Lane?"

The librarian glanced up from her book, her eyes meeting Tammy's. "The little blue cottage, you say? It's a popular place this week. What in particular are you looking for?"

"Any notable events or stories tied to the cottage would be wonderful. You see, I'm a writer, and I find the history of places can provide such rich inspiration for my work."

"Ah, a writer wanting material." One eyebrow raised as she scrutinized Tammy. "Well, I think I can point you in the right direction. In fact, there are some papers and records that might be of interest to you. They're located down this aisle, on the left."

"Thank you."

With a nod of acknowledgment, the woman returned to her book.

Tammy ventured deeper into the library, Lockie jumping ahead, his movements quick and careful to avoid being noticed. She reached the indicated stack and found shelves laden with old newspapers, their pages yellowed by time. History hung in the air, and for a moment, she hesitated, feeling the pull of countless stories waiting to be discovered.

Tammy's fingers hovered over the spines of bound newspapers, their musty scent filling her nostrils. She selected a volume, its weight substantial in her hands. As she opened it, the binding groaned in protest.

"Lockie, do you think we'll find anything?"

He gave her one of his inquisitive stares and waved his tail in response.

Tammy bent closer, her nose almost touching the paper. Headlines from decades past swam before her eyes: "Mayor Cuts Ribbon on New Playground," "Local Boy Wins Spelling Bee." She turned each page with painstaking care, wincing at every rustle and crack.

"Nothing yet." Disappointment crept in. "But there has to be something about our little blue cottage." She massaged her neck, stiffness setting in.

The afternoon light shifted across the library's wooden tables as she worked through volume after volume. The librarian stopped by twice to check on her, curiosity evident in her lingering glances at the stack of bound newspapers.

"Finding anything interesting?" she asked on her second pass.

"Just soaking up the town's everyday happenings."

*What had she meant earlier when she said the cottage was popular this week? Had someone else been asking about it?*

By four o'clock, her eyes burned from squinting at the tiny print. She'd learned about church socials, bridge club championships, and the great debate over whether the town needed a traffic light. Lockie dozed under the table, occasionally stretching or repositioning.

Then "Cedar Lane" came into view. Her finger traced the words, drinking in every detail. Just a mundane notice about road repairs, but it was a start.

With a second wind, Tammy delved into the next volume. She flipped through social announcements, livestock sales, renovation permits, and Help Wanted ads. Each turn transported her further back in time until a June 1954 headline jumped out: "Local Woman Found Dead in Locked Room at the Little Blue Cottage."

"Lockie, look." The cat's eyes flicked up. "We've found our story."

The words blurred as she read them. Mary Collins's body was discovered in the living room—her living room—which was locked from the inside with no weapon present. Goosebumps prickled her skin. *A locked room mystery right under my roof.*

Mary's final moments haunted Tammy—had she seen the knife's glint, met a stranger's eyes, or watched trust shatter beneath a familiar face? The last wound struck close to home. The terror, the killer, the inescapable fate in the cozy room she now took her morning coffee. Did Mary's spirit haunt the cottage?

The shelves loomed, shadows deepening between them. Her breath caught. She forced her eyes back to the yellowed paper.

A grainy photo showed officers clustered at the cottage door—her door.

The library's silence pressed in. No other visible patrons. Tammy shivered.

Was it a crime of passion? A botched break-in? Something more sinister? Was it linked to the threatening letter?

Tammy's eyes slid shut. She felt like a trespasser snooping through the cottage's secrets, like prying into a stranger's diary, but she wanted more. Her hands jittered as she reopened her eyes to the article.

This was only the first discovery. She turned the page forward in time, hungry for answers. Now she had more references to pursue: Mary Collins's name, locked-room puzzle, and murder, which she may have overlooked.

It took two full weeks of daily newspapers before an update appeared: "Mysterious Death in Locked Room Puzzles Sheriff." They were unable to explain how the crime unfolded. The perpetrator vanished into thin air. *Now this is a plot to keep readers up at night.*

The article ended with a plea for information, urging anyone with knowledge to contact the sheriff's department. Someone must have known something?

She continued her research.

*Here's something: "Mysterious Murder Remains Unsolved."*

The article, three months later, stated the truth remained elusive. It described how deputies had combed the area for evidence, but had come up empty-handed. With no leads, the case had gone cold. *How does a locked room murder fade away?* She thought of her novels, where justice was always served, and endings were neatly tied up. Reality was messy.

Tammy leaned back, rubbing her temples. *How had no one witnessed anything? No clues, no suspects, an impossible escape...*

She continued searching, but as the weeks and months went by, it became clear the story had faded from public interest. No new developments emerged in the local paper. The investigation reached a stalemate. On the one-year anniversary, she found a headline: "One Year On, Still No Closure." Then nothing.

Full of disappointment, her curiosity remained unsatiated. A floorboard creaked, startling her. She let out a nervous laugh, realizing it was the old building settling. But the articles had filled her with unease.

Lockie's claws pricked her leg, a gentle reminder of the world beyond musty papers and unsolved mysteries. She scratched his head.

"Okay. Let's update the others."

# Chapter 6

"You won't believe what I found at the library!" Tammy bounded into the bookstore with Lockie strutting at her heels.

Olivia stood at the counter, while Mrs. Temperance appeared from the stacks. They both turned to her as she waved copies of the articles.

"Did you find something?" Olivia asked, her eyes shining as she stepped around the counter.

"There was a murder." Her words came out in a rush as she summarized her findings.

"How dreadful!" said Mrs. Temperance. "And suspicious."

"Unsolved!" Olivia tapped her fingers against her arm. "Who would do such a thing? And how did they escape?"

"The Willow-Crafters came up with nothing. But 1954 is too early for our memories."

Olivia grabbed a notepad from under the counter and shuffled pages. "What was the victim's name?"

"Mary Collins."

"That fits!" said Olivia. "I didn't find anything useful in the local history books, but I discovered the previous owners of the cottage. A Collins family owned the land for generations."

"Should we try to solve it?" Tammy asked. "Our shared passion for mysteries will surely help."

Olivia and Mrs. Temperance exchanged a glance before signaling agreement.

"Very well," Mrs. Temperance said, with a mischievous glint in her eye. "Let's uncover Willowcroft's secrets. Nothing stays buried forever." She shared a meaningful look with Olivia. "Why don't we continue this conversation over breakfast tomorrow? The Swinging Spoon diner makes delightful blueberry pancakes. We can plan our next move."

"Perfect."

Tammy's fingers itched to start mapping theories, connecting dots, and following leads. After years of crafting fictional puzzles, here was a real one—right in her own living room, as if it waited for her arrival. This wasn't research for another novel. This involved real victims, real suspects, and real consequences. That made it nerve-wracking and exhilarating.

Lockie purred as he rubbed against her legs. She smiled down at him.

Olivia gave the cat a scratch. "Eight o'clock?"

As Tammy nodded, Mrs. Temperance clapped her hands. "It's settled." She checked her watch. "My goodness, is that the time? I've got phone calls to make." She opened the door. "Until tomorrow, my dears."

Who was Mary? Who committed such a horrific crime? And most puzzling, how did the killer vanish without a trace?

Olivia broke through Tammy's thoughts. "Don't worry. We'll get to the bottom of this mystery."

"Yes, of course we will. I'm dying to see where this case takes us."

Tammy left the bookstore, her brain churning. A quick stop at Sweet Crumbs next door netted a chicken pot pie for dinner. Her stomach grumbled at the savory scent wafting from the box as she meandered home.

Lockie trotted alongside her. The streets had emptied, save for a scattering of pedestrians hurrying home. None walked in her direction.

A prickle spread across the back of her neck. She glanced over her shoulder but saw nothing out of the ordinary—just the quaint storefronts with their perky window displays that somehow now seemed artificial. She shook her head, trying to dispel her discomfort. *Am I letting all this murder talk get to me? This is*

*Willowcroft, not some crime-ridden city. But Mary Collins probably thought she was safe too...*

"It's your imagination," she muttered. Lockie looked at her, his intense stare deepening her unease.

They passed out of the square. The sound of footsteps made her heart leap into her throat. She quickened her steps, her breath came faster. The footsteps matched her pace. Lockie's ears twitched as he stared behind them.

*Is someone following me?* No. It's just an echo. She spun around, her eyes darting from side to side. The street stretched empty before her, every detail crystal clear in the summer light, exposing her. "Hello?" *Stupid, stupid! You've given away your position. Some writer you are, making rookie mistakes like a plot twist in a dime-store novel.*

No response came, save for the barking of a dog.

Lockie's fur stood on end, his tail puffed. Was it the dog or from something else? Someone else? Tammy's breath came in short gasps as she fought the urge to bolt. The evening summer light made her too visible.

A rhythmic thumping began. Her gut somersaulted. The sound grew louder, closer. She weaponized her keys in her fist—a lesson learned from a self-defense course, a necessary evil in LA. But she would never have walked home at night by herself there. Let's face it—she would never have walked full stop.

Thump. Thump. Thump.

Her palm sweated against the metal keys.

Thump. Thump. Thump.

A teenager emerged from a side street, bouncing a basketball, EarPods in his ears. He strode past Tammy without a glance, too focused on his dribbling. As he reached the end of the block, he took a shot at a hoop mounted above a garage door. The ball swooshed through the net.

She let out a shaky laugh, relief flowing. "It's a kid playing basketball," she muttered to Lockie who had relaxed at her feet. But as the boy disappeared, the silence settled in again, bringing with it a creeping alarm.

She walked faster, almost jogging. *A little further*, Tammy told herself, trying to calm her galloping heart. *Nothing bad ever happens in Willowcroft.* Except to Mary Collins. *Don't think about that now!*

The tree-lined street stretched ahead. The cheerful maples mocked her as they provided perfect hiding spots, their dense summer foliage concealing who-knows-what. Lockie pressed closer to her legs, his tail twitching with each rustle of leaves.

Tammy's imagination conjured movement behind every trunk, every bush. Her breath quickened as she hurried along. Lockie kept pace, peering behind from time to time with flattened ears.

She could see her house now, tantalizingly close. The wind whirred through the trees and carried the faint sound of...footsteps? Again?

Tammy's heart pounded.

She whipped around to confront the follower.

But the street was desolate.

The steps had vanished.

So had her resolve.

Tammy sprinted the last stretch to her cottage, with Lockie a blur of black-and-white fur beside her. They burst through the front door, and Tammy slammed it shut with quaking hands. The deadbolt slid home with a satisfying thunk.

Tammy sagged against the solid wood, her ragged breath and the blood rushing in her ears the only sounds, until her mother took over. "You always trust the wrong people."

Uncertainty crept in, poisoning her newfound friendships. *Could one of them be hiding something? Am I being naive again?* Memories of LA surfaced, intertwining with her present angst. Her boyfriend and her best friend blindsided her within weeks of each other. Her confidence suffocated under the weight of it.

She sank to the floor. *I can't do this. Mom was right.* Tears streamed down her face. Lockie meowed, rubbing against her legs, the soft texture helping to ground her. Doubt gnawed at her with each shaky breath. *I'm not cut out for this.*

But deep within a spark of defiance stirred. She fought back. The writer in her recognized the difference between real danger and manufactured suspense.

Wiping away her tears, she pushed herself to her feet. "I won't let fear control me. I'm not going to let my mother's words or my past define me." *I'm here to change.*

She moved through the house, drawing the curtains against the lingering daylight flooding the rooms with unwanted brilliance. Focusing on the coziness of her cottage soothed some of her insecurities.

She peered through a gap in the curtains, eyes darting back and forth across the empty street. Nothing moved beyond her garden, just the gentle sway of flowers in the soft breeze.

"Do you hear anything, Lockie?"

The cat blinked at her, tail brushing against her legs. His calm demeanor comforted her frayed nerves. Tammy forced a deep breath to aid relaxation. "I'm probably just hearing the wind... Or a raccoon? Nothing sinister." She ran a hand through her hair and let out a shaky laugh.

"I'm being silly. This isn't LA. There's no real danger here." Lockie yawned in response.

Her novels were praised for their masterful tension-building—but now she was doing it to herself, transforming ordinary sounds into threats. Each creak became a footstep, each movement outside a lurker. The very skills that gave her early success were making her jump at a basketball. This was Willowcroft, not some crime-ridden city. Here, the biggest risk was probably tripping over a wayward garden gnome.

She chuckled at the thought, scratching behind Lockie's ears. "Why don't we eat dinner and forget about imaginary stalkers?"

His answering meow sounded like agreement. Tammy moved down the hall, her legs shaky but her mind clearer. She kicked off her shoes. The tranquil surroundings of the cottage steadied her jangled nerves. Lockie padded after her into the kitchen, where Tammy busied herself making a cup of chamomile tea and reheating the pie.

As the kettle whistled, the last of her tension ebbed away. She poured the boiling water over the tea bag, inhaling the nourishing aroma. Through the kitchen window, the sun painted everything in golden light. No lurking danger. She shook her head, chuckling at her earlier panic. "Some mystery expert I am, jumping at shadows like a character in a bad horror movie." Soft fur wound around her ankles.

Tammy carried her mug and plate to the living room. She settled onto the couch, pulling a soft throw over her legs. Lockie hopped up beside her, kneading her leg, then curling into a contented ball. Tammy sipped her tea, letting its heat spread through her before digging into the pie.

The best way to end the jitters is to solve the case. Tammy read and re-read the articles hoping a clue would jump out at her. But her concentration was broken by Lockie perking up. His ears twitched, and he turned his head toward the opposite wall. She ignored him, wanting to stay focused, but he let out a growl as he leaped from the sofa and slunk across the room, fixing his gaze upon a threat invisible to Tammy. His back arched and his fur bristled before he scratched and hissed at the area between the fireplace and the bookshelf, determined to get at something.

"What's gotten into you?" She set aside the pages and inspected what had captured Lockie's attention. Staring at the innocuous spot, she saw nothing to explain the cat's behavior. Was there more to it than met the eye? Was it connected to the murder? The idea seemed farfetched.

"If there's something hidden here, we'll find it."

Tammy examined the bookshelves housing her recently unpacked novel collection. She pressed the wood in a systematic exploration for concealed triggers that might reveal an unseen door or passage. She scrutinized every nook and cranny with painstaking precision. She had never considered checking for levers or switches before unpacking.

Despite her thorough search, she found no trace of anything unusual or out of place. Reality sank in; a secret room wasn't plausible with the kitchen directly behind. What had drawn the cat's attention?

Tammy stepped back, confused. Lockie continued to paw at the wall, his tail whipping back and forth. A cold dread gripped her as a sinister thought formed. What if he wasn't reacting to something physical, but something...supernatural?

She shook her head, trying to dismiss the notion. Ghosts weren't real. Were they? But with Lockie's intense focus on that spot, she remembered Mary was murdered in the room. Her skin prickled with goosebumps.

She'd read enough mysteries to be aware supernatural events usually had rational causes. But as the room grew colder, she questioned her certainties. Tammy hugged herself, rubbing her arms to ward off the sudden chill. Did her breath fog in the air? Lockie let out a low, mournful yowl as the hair on the back of her neck stood up.

"Mary?"

She scanned the room, half expecting to see a translucent figure materialize.

"If you're here, Mary, we want to find out what happened to you."

A gust of wind rattled the windows, making Tammy jump. They were closed, weren't they? She hurried over to check, her hands trembling as she tugged at the locks. They were secure.

She crouched beside Lockie, running her hand along his bristling fur. His demeanor changed. He gave one final sniff before padding back to the couch as if it were no big deal.

"What was that all about? Are you now telling me there's nothing there?" He started to purr.

*I'm going to have to decide whether I believe in ghosts or not. For future reference.*

Tammy shook it off and returned her attention to the articles. As she read late into the night, Lockie remained by her side, his eyes occasionally darting around the room as if he was tracking something invisible to her. She reached down to pet him, drawing comfort from his presence. "We'll get to the bottom of this."

Her eyes roamed the room. What secrets did these walls hold?

# Chapter 7

The scent of sizzling bacon and maple syrup enveloped her as she stepped into the Swinging Spoon. Her eyes swept the diner, taking in the red booths and chrome accents that transported her back to the 1950s. The jukebox crooned a cheerful melody, lending a whimsical backdrop to their gathering.

"Over here!" Olivia said over the diner's chatter. Tammy spotted her waving from a booth and slid in next to her, the vinyl squeaking beneath her.

Mrs. Temperance sat across from them.

Tammy's stomach knotted with keenness and trepidation. "Are we doing this?" The prospect of diving into a real-life mystery was thrilling yet daunting.

Olivia adjusted her glasses and bent forward. "I think we should. We have the passion for solving mysteries and oodles of curiosity."

"Don't forget about justice, dear," said Mrs. Temperance.

"If we don't uncover the truth, who will?" asked Olivia.

Tammy's grip tightened on the edge of the table, drawing strength from the cool chrome beneath her fingers. Her mind flashed to Lockie's strange behavior and the unsettling events around her house and garden. The words teetered on the tip of her tongue but stalled there. Trust was still a fragile thing, and the idea of revealing too much too soon made her hesitate.

For now, she decided, focusing on the murder was the best course of action. If the eerie happenings proved relevant, she could share them later.

She caught Olivia's gaze and saw the fire of determination reflected there. Unanswered questions and hidden secrets flashed through her mind. With a steady breath, her need for answers won out. "You're right. We can't walk away from this."

The clink of ceramic on Formica made them all jump. A server in a pink uniform dress and comically large black glasses appeared, coffeepot in hand. "Coffee, anyone? Plenty to go around."

"Yes, please," they chorused, as dark liquid streamed into their mugs.

"Peggy," Mrs. Temperance said, gesturing toward Tammy, "this is our new resident and friend, Tammy. Tammy, meet Peggy, the owner of this fine establishment."

Peggy bowed her head, her hands too full to offer a handshake. "Welcome to town, Tammy. Now, what can I get you ladies to eat this morning?"

As Tammy read the menu, her companions ordered with the ease of regulars.

"I'll have the Belgian waffle with fresh strawberries and whipped cream, please," said Olivia.

"The classic eggs benedict for me," said Mrs. Temperance.

"French toast, thanks," said Tammy.

The door jingled, and Mrs. Temperance's face lit up. "Ah, here they are!"

Tammy turned around to see two males entering. A lanky teenager, eyes glued to his smartphone, stumbled in, followed by a confident older man.

"The usual, gentlemen?" Peggy asked.

"Yes, thank you, ma'am," they both responded.

"One full American and one pancake stack coming up."

The two newcomers slid next to Mrs. Temperance, who set down her coffee. "Tammy, I have the pleasure of introducing you to two allies who will be instrumental in our investigation. This is Xander, a tech-savvy young man on summer vacation, and Mr. Wallace, Wally to his friends, a retired detective with decades of experience." She gestured to each in turn, but Xander's eyes remained glued to his smartphone while Wally gave a polite nod. *Was she ready for more new people?*

"These two were also involved in last week's great bear caper," said Olivia.

"I was first," said Mrs. Temperance. "The bear licked my kitchen window!"

"I was next," said Wally. "A hulking bear scratched at my front door."

Olivia sat tall. "Then it was my turn with the bear breaking my store's window."

"The perp took photos at each bear attack and emailed them to the newspaper office," said Wally.

"That's where I came in!" piped up Xander. "I hacked into email records and found proof it was sent by Nick Bradley from school!"

"With Mrs. Temperance identifying the honey, and with my CCTV footage, Nick couldn't deny his involvement," said Olivia.

"Yes, he orchestrated the whole thing because he was bored during summer vacation," said Mrs. Temperance, shaking her head.

"He'll be doing community service for the rest of his life if I have anything to do with it," said Wally, a fierce resolve in his eyes.

Olivia patted Wally's hand. "If you see a teenager sweeping the square or picking up trash, it's most likely Nick. It's sheriff-mandated activities, instead of being charged and having a record."

Peggy arrived with the food and Tammy's mouth watered at the sight of the delicious plates.

As the server walked away, Tammy said, "Looks like I have some catching up to do in the investigation department. I only make up mysteries." *Although, the haunted hotel on my road trip was a mystery. Does that count?*

"That sounds like the perfect experience if you ask me," said Olivia. "I've read all your books and I never solve it before the end."

Tammy appreciated the feedback and confidence boost. *What do reviewers know?* "Thank you for letting me join your team."

"Speaking of which," Mrs. Temperance leaned in, "shall we talk about our case? I caught the boys up last night when I telephoned them."

The group chatted away as they ate their breakfasts. Tammy smiled as she scanned the booth. This was happening—they were banding together to solve a mystery.

Lockie leaped onto the table, making everyone jump. "Lockie!" Heat flared in her cheeks as the feline knocked over the sugar dispenser.

Olivia stifled a laugh while other diner patrons gasped and the staff exchanged irritated glances.

"Did you follow me into town?" Tammy asked, keeping calm despite her mortification.

Mrs. Temperance patted him on the head, her face softening with affection. "He's been wandering about for days now. It's no surprise he found his way here."

"Shoo, get away!" Peggy hurried over, grabbing Lockie around the middle. The cat wiggled in her grasp.

Tammy reached out to take the squirming cat. "I'm so sorry." Before she secured him, Lockie twisted free and leaped back onto the table, his tail lashing.

Peggy placed her hands on her hips, her brow furrowed. "Now listen here. We can't have cats scampering around my diner. It violates health codes, and it'll scare away customers."

Tammy's embarrassment deepened. "I understand. I'll take him outside right away."

Lockie had other ideas. He turned his attention to Peggy, sitting on the table and fixing her with wide, innocent green eyes. He let out a soft, plaintive meow, causing Peggy to hesitate.

The cat hopped down and rubbed against Peggy's legs, purring louder than usual. Peggy eyed the cat for a moment, her hands still perched on her hips. "Oh, it's you..." The deep lines on the server's face softened. "I suppose since he did help catch the troublemaker. But just this once."

Tammy turned to Mrs. Temperance. "The prankster you mentioned when we met—*he* was responsible for the bear visits, and *Lockie* caught him."

"Yes, dear," Mrs. Temperance replied with a casual wave.

Peggy crouched to scratch Lockie behind the ears. "Okay, he can stay given his good deed." The cat arched into her touch, his purrs growing louder. Peggy's stern demeanor melted away as she fell under his spell. "As long as he behaves himself."

Tammy glanced around the diner where patrons had mixed reactions. Some were amused, while others frowned and crossed their arms, their expressions tightening at the sight of the feline.

Lockie leaped onto the seat back cushion next to Tammy, curling up. He stared at the group with an air of contentment, as if declaring, "I'm one of you now."

Tammy chuckled at the cat's antics. "Lockie has won over Peggy's heart." She reached out and gave a gentle pat. "I guess he's officially part of the investigation team."

Wally eyed the cat. "Reckon he might be useful, having a nose for clues and all. He did catch Nick."

"How did Lockie help in the bear caper?" Tammy asked.

"Nick ran when the sheriff went to talk to him," said Wally, "and a stray cat, who now seems to be called Lockie, came out of nowhere, tripping him, allowing Deputy Brown to apprehend the lad. He became quite the celebrity."

"He can be our mascot," Olivia suggested.

"Or our secret weapon," Xander added with a smirk.

Surrounded by this group of quirky, passionate people—and one extraordinary feline—Tammy's confidence expanded. In less than a week, she had met more people than in her first year at her LA apartment.

"Okay, here's what I'm thinking," said Tammy. "We each have our own strengths. I'll head back to the library." *Focus on the facts of the murder and nothing else.*

Olivia piped up. "My genealogy side gig comes with access to various databases. Between helping customers at the store, I can search for leads."

"Great idea," Wally nodded. "I'll see how far my connections can get me with the sheriff. I might be able to get a peek at the original case file."

"I'm visiting the nursing home this afternoon," said Mrs. Temperance. "The town's oldest residents might recall something."

"Count me in for online sleuthing," Xander said, adjusting his glasses. "One digital footprint coming right up." He gave a mock salute.

"Remember, we're talking seventy years ago," Mrs. Temperance said. "Social media didn't exist in the 1950s."

"I don't know how you survived. I'll focus on other digital archives," his fingers already flying across the screen.

Tammy smirked as she caught Mrs. Temperance and Wally exchanging amused glances, their shared eye roll not going unnoticed.

"It's perfect," said Tammy. "We all bring something unique to this. We're going to crack this case wide open!"

"Absolutely," Olivia said, smiling at the group. "We're a fantastic team who'll bring justice to Mary Collins."

"Here's to teamwork and camaraderie," Mrs. Temperance declared, lifting her cup in a toast.

"Cheers!" they exclaimed, clinking their cups.

As they continued to eat and discuss their plans, a sense of unity enveloped the group. Wally's intense gaze met hers, conveying determination.

Olivia angled her body toward the others, her animated hand gestures emphasizing each point she made.

Xander alternated between tapping on his phone and fidgeting with the hem of his shirt, his shoulders hunched in. Mrs. Temperance, ever composed, said, "Let's remember discretion is key, dears. We don't want to alert the suspect or anyone who might be involved."

"Agreed," they murmured in unison. Lockie pricked his ears.

"Mrs. Temperance is right," said Olivia. "We need to be as stealthy as Lockie here." She offered the cat a smile which he returned with a slow blink.

Xander looked up from his phone. "You don't think the killer's still alive, do you? This happened seventy years ago, so they'd be ninety or older."

"People can live into their nineties, even reach one hundred," Mrs. Temperance pointed out.

"And some can even drive," Wally added with a chuckle. "I can't wait to wreak havoc when I'm ninety and on my mobility scooter."

"You don't want to upset someone on a mobility scooter," joked Mrs. Temperance as she patted Xander's hand. "They might run over you."

"Watch out for those speed demons on wheels," said Wally as he turned an imaginary steering wheel. "You can't out maneuver those zippy vehicles when they have you in their sights!"

"At five miles an hour?" Olivia said, "That's the slowest hit-and-run in history!"

"It's a race against time and battery life," Tammy added, and the group burst into giggles.

"Ah, the joys of aging," said Mrs. Temperance.

As the laughter subsided, Wally brought the conversation back to the investigation. "But seriously, we can't rule out the possibility the killer is still alive. Even if they aren't, there might be someone who has been keeping secrets all these years."

Wally lay back in his seat, his eyes narrowing. "I've seen cases where the truth comes out decades later. Sometimes it's a deathbed confession, or a long-lost piece of evidence resurfaces, like your letter, Tammy. We need to be prepared for anything."

*Prepared for anything*. She gulped, realizing this wasn't just about solving an old mystery anymore—it could become dangerous.

Agreement was expressed by all, Wally's detective experience a clear advantage for the team. "We should keep our meetings regular but inconspicuous, to be safe."

Olivia broke everyone's thoughts by gathering her belongings in a flurry of activity and shuffling past Tammy to exit the booth. "I have to open the store, but do come by with your discoveries. The back room is always available. It can be our secret lair and help me be involved even while working. There's a door disguised as a bookshelf between the true crime and esoteric books."

A secret lair and a hidden door? Olivia's suggestion was so perfectly characteristic of her eccentric and resourceful nature. Everyone could participate without raising suspicions, and their base would be hidden behind a bookshelf in a bookstore. This setup was straight out of her childhood fantasies.

"Crime and esoteric doesn't sound like the Dewey Decimal system," said Xander.

"It's not. That's for libraries. Look, walking into a store is not suspicious. If you come in separately and sometimes use the back door, no one would suspect a thing!" She hurried out the door after a near miss with a server carrying a tray of milkshakes.

With the shakes safe, Mrs. Temperance said, "At the end of each day, we can touch base at the store, share findings, and plan our next steps."

"Sounds good to me," Xander said, his fingers busy. "This is going to be the best summer vacation ever!"

As they wrapped up their discussion, Tammy marveled at how drastically her life had changed since leaving LA less than two weeks ago. Instead of sitting trapped in her noisy apartment after being abandoned by her boyfriend, she was now surrounded by new friends, immersed in fresh hobbies, and on the brink of new adventures. Moving to Willowcroft was proving to be a great decision. With renewed energy, she said, "Let's get to work."

Tammy caught Wally's eye as he stood, his face mirroring her own energy. Even Mrs. Temperance seemed to have an extra spring in her step as she rose. They were ready to chase down leads. Xander remained seated, given his investigation had already started.

# Chapter 8

Hazel Temperance hummed to herself as she measured ingredients for making scones. Years of practice had taught her weathered hands to cut the butter and rub it into the flour. She added milk with a hint of vanilla essence and lemon juice into the middle of the now crumb-like mixture. As a soft dough formed, Hazel became lost in the simple pleasure of her craft.

As she worked, memories of her childhood surfaced, vivid and comforting. Her mother regaled her with stories of life in wartime England and her romance with an American GI. After the war, she had moved to Willowcroft, bringing her English traditions with her. Scones, always served with thick cream and sweet, chunky jam, were a staple in their home.

A stickler for tradition, she would frown at any mention of "jelly," insisting, "Jelly is a different thing entirely." That familiar voice guided Hazel's hands through the process.

"Always remember, my dear," she had said, "the secret to a perfect scone is not just in the ingredients, but in the care you put into each step."

With those words in her heart, Hazel lovingly shaped the dough into delicate rounds before placing them on a baking sheet lined with parchment paper. They glistened after the rich egg wash was applied.

Today, there was an added purpose behind each step. Her famous scones needed to get loose lips talking about the past by the residents at the local nursing home, Serenity Gardens.

Hazel slid the tray into the oven. While they baked, she tidied, wiping counters and washing dishes. The aroma of fresh scones soon permeated the house.

When the timer chimed, she removed the golden nuggets from the oven. Leaving them to cool, she turned her attention to her wardrobe.

"Let's see now." She rifled through her extensive collection. Each piece matched a specific mood, and she took pride in her eclectic assortment. Today, the vibrant purple shawl adorned with embroidered birds along the hem called her. It reflected her eccentric style and eye for beauty. She draped it around herself, admiring the way it framed her face in the mirror.

With her outfit complete, Hazel returned to the kitchen where she packed the scones into a wicker basket with care. Beside them, she nestled a container of cream and a jar of her homemade strawberry jam—a recent batch she had made using the ripest berries from her garden. The sweet, fruity aroma tantalized her senses, and she imagined the delight of the nursing home residents enjoying the treat. For Hazel, sharing food and forming meaningful friendships were life's great joys.

"Ah, now we're all set," she said, clasping the basket's lid shut. She pictured the faces she might encounter. What tales would they spin? Was one of them hiding a sinister secret? Would she meet a murderer? She shuddered.

Hazel reminded herself every person had a story worth telling—some darker than others. She gathered her things and headed out the door, ready to face whatever came her way.

Serenity Gardens sat a few blocks from her house. She admired the historic homes along the way with their well-tended flowers.

Upon arriving, Nurse Emma, sporting a fabulous pair of scrubs adorned with cut avocados, greeted Hazel at the front desk. Hazel regarded her as a kindred spirit, both known for their quirky attire—Emma with her whimsical scrub designs and Hazel with her riotous cascade of colorful shawls.

The nurse's face lit up. "Good morning, Mrs. Temperance! It's lovely to see you."

"Thank you, dear."

Mrs. Temperance recognized the familiar scent of disinfectant from the days when she helped Harold clean his medical equipment.

A young man brushed past after entering behind her. Emma acknowledged him. "Hello Nathan, here to visit your grandfather again so soon?"

Nathan glanced at the nurse without stopping, offering a sarcastic smirk in reply. His shoulders were hitched close to his ears as he disappeared. What had brought such concern to a young man?

"Ah, well." The nurse sighed, turning back to Hazel. "Now, how can I help you today?"

She patted her basket. "I've brought some treats to share. And I was hoping to speak with some of the residents who may remember Willowcroft during the 1950s. I'm trying to uncover the town's history."

"Of course. Let me introduce you to a few people who might be in the mood for a chat and a treat."

Emma led her down a sterile, door-lined hallway. She tightened her grip on the basket, willing the scones' aroma to mask the mothball scent teasing her nose. Residents in wheelchairs rolled past while the soft shuffling of walkers filled her ears.

Would this place one day become her home—the final chapter of her story? She cherished the house she'd shared with her late husband, the town's last local doctor. Their beloved home held memories in every corner, laughter whispered through the rooms. The idea of leaving it was as daunting as it was inevitable. Time marched on, relentless. How much longer could she manage on her own?

Emma stopped at a doorway and gestured inside. "Mrs. Temperance, this is Mr. Hill. He lived in Willowcroft for a good portion of his life and might have some stories to tell."

"Hello, Mr. Hill." Hazel extended her hand.

The elderly man lifted his gaze from his jigsaw puzzle, grasping her hand with an unexpected firm grip. "Nice to meet you, ma'am."

"Mr. Hill, I'm hoping you can help me uncover some of Willowcroft's history from the 1950s. Do you mind if I ask you a few questions? I have home-baked scones to share." Hazel revealed the contents of her basket.

Mr. Hill gestured toward a nearby chair. "How delicious. I'd be happy to help."

Mrs. Temperance settled in as the sweet aroma of fresh scones spread through the room. Mr. Hill licked his lips as she handed him a still warm scone.

"Thank you kindly, ma'am," he said, taking a bite. "Mmm, these are divine."

Mrs. Temperance loved seeing people appreciate her baking. "Our town has such a rich history. I'd love to hear your recollections from the 1950s." Her unhurried words were meant to invite him to share. "Do you remember anything remarkable? Something that stood out?"

Mr. Hill's forehead crinkled as he searched his memories while chewing. "The fifties were my teenage years. I was pretty wrapped up in myself back then."

"How about the name Mary Collins?"

"Mary Collins, you say? The name does ring a bell," he licked cream from the corner of his mouth, "but nothing specific comes to mind... Wait, the old Collins farm was on Cedar Lane."

"That's right," Hazel moved forward on the seat.

"But there hasn't been a Collins family in Willowcroft for decades. I don't recall when they left. The McLeods live out there now." He took another bite of his scone.

Mr. Hill's rheumy eyes lit up. "Oh, I do remember something about the Collins farm." He shifted toward Mrs. Temperance, the scent of peppermint and tobacco wafting between them. "There was quite a commotion when the McLeods bought that property."

Mrs. Temperance straightened, her interest piqued. "Oh? What kind of commotion?" She strove for composure, not wanting to betray her eagerness.

His wrinkled face deepened with concentration, his thick, bushy eyebrows drawing into a tight V. "I walked past the little blue cottage one evening and saw a real heated argument going on in the front yard."

"Did you hear what they were arguing about?" Her fingers tightened around her pen. Her pulse thrummed in her throat.

Mr. Hill shook his head, his jowls quivering. "There was a lot of shouting and arm waving. It was mighty strange. The Collins family had owned that land for generations. It wasn't like them to cause a fuss."

Mrs. Temperance's mind raced. Did this relate to Mary Collins's murder? Her pen dashed across the notepad, her handwriting scrawled in her fervor. "Do you remember anything they said?"

He paused, lifting his scone to his mouth. Mrs. Temperance held her breath, willing him to recall more. Mr. Hill took a slow, deliberate bite, crumbs catching in his white mustache.

"You know, I always wondered if that argument had something to do with..." he trailed off, frustration clouding his features. "Oh, drat. Can't quite remember what I was going to say."

Mrs. Temperance damped down her disappointment with a slow exhale. She maintained her composure, hoping his memory would return, but he just shook his head and returned his attention to his half-eaten scone.

With a slight tremor in her hand, she underlined, "McLeod farm purchase and heated argument." Did she have a potential lead? She craved more. She glanced at Mr. Hill, noting the faraway expression on his face. One more try.

"Mr. Hill." Mrs. Temperance reached out to pat his gnarled hand. His papery skin shifted under her touch. "What about 1954? Does that year spark any memories?" If the murder didn't come to mind, she thought there was no point in mentioning it unless she had to.

He eased back in his chair, his eyes growing distant and thoughtful. "1954... Was that the year the drive-in opened?" He paused and gave Hazel a playful wink. "I stole my first kiss at the drive-in."

Heat spread over her face before she realized he had priorities other than murder in 1954.

"Well, Mr. Hill, I appreciate you taking the time to chat with me. Your memories offer a delightful glimpse into Willowcroft's past."

"It's been a pleasure, Mrs. Temperance. Your scones were a real treat, and thank you for the little trip to the good old days."

Hazel entered the corridor and caught Emma's attention. "Who's next?"

"Was Mr. Hill helpful?"

"I think he started to flirt with me." Despite the decades separating them, the pair giggled like two schoolgirls sharing a secret.

The nurse led Hazel to the common room. Another resident sat in a plush arm-chair, his weathered hands clasped in his lap. His eyes, framed by deep wrinkles, sparkled with curiosity as Hazel approached.

"Mr. Andrews, this is Mrs. Temperance. She's interested in learning more about Willowcroft in the 1950s. And she has scones."

He straightened his posture. "Ah, the 1950s, hey. Those were the days. Please, have a seat." He gestured to the empty chair beside him, his eyes lingering on the basket.

Hazel sat and prepared a scone. "Mr. Andrews, I've always been fascinated by the stories of our town's past. I was hoping you might be able to share some memories from that time, particularly 1954, if possible."

"1954, you say? Let me think." His gaze drifted upward, searching the depths of his mind as he chewed.

Hazel's breath caught with anticipation, each chew holding the promise of uncovering buried history.

"Well, I do remember something. That was the inaugural Michigan Week celebration. It was quite the spectacle, showcasing all the wonderful things our state had to offer. Parades, festivals, special events all week long."

He paused, a flicker of uncertainty crossing his features. He dropped to a conspiratorial whisper. "But there was something else, wasn't there? Something that had the whole town buzzing with speculation and rumors."

Hazel gripped the edge of her seat. Could this be a clue to what happened to Mary Collins? "What was it, Mr. Andrews? Can you remember?"

But just as the recollection appeared, it vanished. His eyes grew distant, his lucidity slipping away like the tail end of a dream. "I'm so happy to visit my grandma today," he said, a childlike enthusiasm replacing his earlier seriousness. "She gives me sweets."

Hazel's heart sank, yet she maintained her composure. She spread generous dollops of jam and cream on a fresh scone and handed it to Mr. Andrews, hoping it would bring him some comfort in place of his grandma's candy. "Enjoy this. And have a lovely visit with your gran."

Emma caught Hazel's eye from across the room, giving a gentle head tilt toward Mrs. Lewis, who was nestled in a chair by the window.

Mrs. Lewis started off strong with her chatter, but soon her memories fragmented like those of the other residents. "I remember the soda fountain at the pharmacy... and the memorial in the town square..." she rambled, her recollections slipping away. Hazel sifted through the details, finding nothing of use. Her spirit dampened.

She carried her basket through the hall, her mind turning over the snippets of conversation. A heated argument at the cottage. The McLeods buying the property... Was there a deeper connection? She had hoped for more. Her shoulders slumped.

She was about to turn away when the nurse stopped her.

"Mrs. Bennett's having a good day if you've got time for one more?"

Hazel's heart lifted a little. She glanced at Emma, seeing the understanding in her eyes, and felt a flicker of gratitude for the nurse's thoughtfulness.

"Why not? There are two lucky scones left. One for her and one for me."

They walked along a corridor lined with paintings different from the rest of the halls. She paused at each one. The serene landscapes and vibrant still lifes captured the essence of Willowcroft.

"Mrs. Bennett is quite the artist," the nurse remarked, noticing Hazel's interest. "They're all her work."

"Truly?" Hazel replied, impressed. "She's very talented."

As they entered the room, Mrs. Bennett sat by the window, her gentle gaze lost in thought. Short, white hair framed her face, accentuating her delicate features.

"Mrs. Bennett," Emma called. "I'd like you to meet someone. This is Mrs. Temperance. She's been talking with some of our residents today, and I thought you two might enjoy each other's company."

"Hello, Mrs. Bennett. It's a pleasure to meet you."

"Likewise," the woman replied.

"I believe we might have a friend in common."

Mrs. Bennett's gaze rested on Hazel.

"Marjorie Hubbard is part of my knitting circle. I've heard her mention your name."

"Ah, yes, Marjorie. She checks on me from time to time. Such a good girl."

Hazel had to stifle a scoff. She knew Marjorie as a girl and good she was not. She'd teased both Betty and Hazel throughout their school years.

"Would you care for a scone, dear?" She pulled one of the remaining pastries from her basket. "I made them fresh today, and they're simply divine with strawberry jam."

"That sounds delicious."

Hazel spread a scoop of her homemade jam onto Mrs. Bennett's scone, followed by cream. "Emma mentioned you're quite the artist. The paintings outside your room are exquisite."

"Thank you," Mrs. Bennett replied, her eyes lighting up as she spoke of her passion. "I've always found solace in painting—capturing the beauty surrounding us and preserving it on canvas."

As they continued to chat, Hazel steered the conversation toward Willowcroft's history, hoping Mrs. Bennett might have some insights or memories to share. To her delight, it seemed she might be lucky this time.

Mrs. Bennett launched into tales of her childhood adventures around town—climbing trees, swimming in the creek, getting into mischief with friends and her brother. Her eyes drifted.

Hazel asked Mrs. Bennett to recall the 1950s specifically.

"I turned eleven in 1950. I could tell you a thing or two."

"Do you remember—"

A shadow fell across the doorway, and Hazel turned to see the young man from earlier, his arms crossed, leaning against the doorframe. His unyielding gaze was pinned on Mrs. Bennett, as though daring her to falter.

Mrs. Bennett froze, her hands fluttering as she dropped the scone. Her face paled, her lips trembled as she stared at Nathan with wide eyes. She hugged herself tightly.

"Mrs. Bennett..." Hazel bent closer and reached her hand out. There was something about his unflinching glare that made her stomach tighten. "Is everything all right?"

Mrs. Bennett's eyes darted between Nathan and the window. "No more! I won't say another word!" She refused to make eye contact with Hazel.

*What just happened?* "Please, Mrs. Bennett, I didn't mean to upset you," said Hazel, trying to salvage their conversation. She glanced at Nathan.

But it was too late. Mrs. Bennett had retreated behind an impenetrable wall, shutting out Hazel and any further discussion of the town's history. It was clear something about Nathan's presence had rattled her, but why?

"Perhaps we can speak another time," Hazel suggested, hoping to leave the door open for future conversations.

"I'm not saying anything," Mrs. Bennett yelled.

At the determination in Mrs. Bennett's voice, Hazel rose from her seat with a nagging unease. Nathan had moved on, but the tension lingered.

Emma hurried in at the commotion. "I'm so sorry. She has these episodes sometimes. Her dementia comes and goes. I think it's best we end the visit here."

Hazel nodded, frustration prickling. She would have to unravel this mystery another day. For now, any secrets Mrs. Bennett knew would remain locked away.

The nurse tried to soothe Mrs. Bennett. "Let's take some deep breaths, okay?" She guided Mrs. Bennett in slow inhales and exhales.

*Did I cause this?* But it was Nathan's intense scowl at Mrs. Bennett that gnawed at Hazel.

Emma turned to Hazel. "I apologize. I thought today was a good day for Mrs. Bennett, but it seems her dementia may be progressing faster than we anticipated."

"Please don't worry," Hazel replied, gentle yet firm. "I understand these things can be unpredictable. Focus on helping her settle."

With Mrs. Bennett calm but holding a vacant stare, Hazel said, "That boy...his presence upset her for some reason. Who is he?"

"That's Nathan. He visits his grandfather often. I'm afraid he can be rather rude at times. But we've never seen him provoke a reaction from Mrs. Bennett before."

Hazel absorbed this information with a pensive frown. There was more to unravel about this. She left the nursing home and walked along the familiar path. The scent of flowers wafted through the air as she pondered the details of the encounter—the change in Mrs. Bennett's demeanor, Nathan's cold gaze, and the secrets behind them.

There was more to this, and her clever young friends would want to hear about it.

# Chapter 9

Wally entered the sheriff's building through the side entry meant for employees only. He'd have to sweet-talk Beverly, the formidable records clerk, into letting him access the basement archives.

"Come on, Bev," Wally cajoled, flashing his most charming smile at the stern-faced woman. "It's for a good cause. I wouldn't ask if it wasn't important."

She pursed her lips, her eyes narrowing behind her cat-eye glasses. "There are rules, *Mr.* Wallace. Those files are confidential. I can't let any old body go poking around."

"But I'm not just anyone, am I?"

"You are no longer Sheriff Wallace now, are you?" Why did she have to be the only one in town to drop "sheriff" from his name?

Wally pulled out the bunch of flowers he had hidden.

"Good heavens," she said, her face softening at the sight of the bouquet. "How beautiful..." But she swiftly regained her composure. "How dare you think you can buy me with flowers, *retired* sheriff."

"Aren't they lovely? Imagine them on your desk brightening your workday."

"You and your Boston charm." She made a tsk sound and tapped her pen. "Fine. But you didn't get this from me, you hear?" She passed a key to Wally. "And don't go making a mess. Eddie's finishing organizing those files now."

Wally grinned, reaching across to squeeze her hand. "You're a peach, Bev. I owe you one."

"You're going to have to get past Eddie, too." She gave him a disapproving glare, as if to say Wally's charms wouldn't work on him. Wally had other plans for Eddie.

He descended the slick vinyl stairs, the archives key heavy in his hand. The gate was locked—good. Maybe he wouldn't have to use his card with Eddie after all. He navigated the rows of metal shelves until he reached the section labeled "Unsolved Cases."

Out of nowhere, a hand touched his shoulder, making him jump. "Wally," called out a voice. Wally turned, his sudden jerk causing Eddie's coffee mug to overturn and spill brown liquid on the floor. "Careful. You're out of practice. You left the gate unlocked. Otherwise, I never would have known you were here."

Rookie mistake. He'd have to do better.

"What brings you into the dungeon?"

Wally chuckled, clapping his old colleague on the back. "Eddie, my friend, how about helping an old-timer out? I'm looking into a cold case from '54."

Eddie's eyebrows shot up. "What's got you digging up ancient history?"

"Let's just say I'm trying to keep the old gray matter ticking over so it doesn't get stale." He winked. "Any chance you'd point me to those files?"

Eddie scratched his chin. "Well, those records are for current employees only. But for you…" He glanced around before continuing in a hushed tone. "Remember when you covered my shift the night of my daughter's dance recital?"

This was shaping up to be easier than he thought.

"Consider this me returning the favor." Eddie led the way deeper into the shelves, stopping at a filing cabinet. "Here we are."

He went to open the top drawer when Wally stopped him. "Hey, it's best if you don't see the exact case."

Eddie stepped aside. "Good thinking. If I don't know, I can't tell anyone. I didn't see anything, and you were never here. I'll go clean the coffee spill."

"I owe you one."

Without looking, Eddie backed into a box teetering on the edge of a shelf behind him. Papers scattered across the room and under the shelves as the two men scrambled to collect them. They stuffed the pages haphazardly into the file and replaced the box.

Wally waited as Eddie walked away and disappeared before accessing the cabinet. It creaked, the metal scraping against the tracks to reveal yellowed folders. He flicked through the faded labels, seeking the right year, the right case. *1954, 1954, where are you?*

And then it appeared. "Collins, Mary. Homicide." The folder was thin, belying the weight of the mystery within. Wally slid it from the drawer, his hands twitching as he held it. He glanced over his shoulder, checking if anyone was there. Beverly and Eddie had let him slip by this time, but one misstep and his past life in law enforcement would mean nothing. Leaving quickly was his best option.

He tucked the precious folder into his satchel, strode out of the archives, up the stairs, and left the key on Beverly's unattended desk. His heart pounded as he hurried out, desperate to dig into the folder.

Less than five minutes later, since his house was three doors from the side exit of the building, Wally was sitting at his kitchen table rifling through the onionskin pages. "Good grief," he muttered. "This file looks like it's been dropped and reshuffled more times than a casino deck of cards."

Wally sifted through the chaos of seventy years of dust and disorganization. He skimmed the autopsy report: "Victim sustained a single wound. Time of death estimated approximately 7 p.m. on June 27th, 1954."

The words sank in as Wally turned to the grainy, ghostlike photographs tucked inside the folder. A figure lay crumpled on the floor, frozen in black and white. *Note to self: don't let Tammy see these.*

# Chapter 10

Tammy clutched her research as she worked her way to the back shelves of Olivia's bookstore. Her fingers danced over spines as she feigned casual interest in the embossed titles promising adventure and romance. The scent of ink mingled with a jasmine candle Olivia had burning on the counter.

Lockie, ever the curious feline, meowed before pawing at one peculiar section. His green eyes glinted with playful intent as he nudged his head toward an almost imperceptible gap nestled between two bookcases. Was this it? The secret entrance into the back room?

Tammy pressed against the polished wood. It gave way with a soft creak. She stifled a giggle, casting cautious glances around to ensure they remained undetected. It was like stepping into Narnia.

She pushed further and Lockie disappeared through the gap. With a swift motion, Tammy slipped through, entering the back room. She wasn't accustomed to such clandestine behavior, but found it exhilarating.

"Welcome to our lair," came from behind her, making Tammy jump.

She turned to face her new friend, who wore a cheeky grin after sneaking in. "How did you—"

"Sorry. I couldn't resist a bit of mystery flair. Make yourself at home. I'll join you as soon as I can."

Tammy glanced around the multifunctional room. A large, sturdy table dominated, its surface scarred with scratches and ink stains—a testament to years of use. To her left, boxes with flaps askew held books awaiting their place on the shelves.

Along the right-hand wall sat a mini kitchen. The compact space featured a simple benchtop with a microwave, coffeemaker, and mismatched mugs. The overhead cupboards, their doors ajar, revealed snacks and supplies. She imagined Olivia here, brewing a fresh cup of coffee during a lull in the bookstore—a brief respite on a busy day.

A back door offered an alternative entry point and a staircase at the far end disappeared into the shadows, no doubt leading to Olivia's apartment. The whole area was cozy, efficient, and charming—much like its owner.

A soft meow came from Lockie. "Let's get set up before the others arrive." She unfurled her research across the tabletop.

The store's bell tinkled, and Mrs. Temperance peeked around the bookcase, her purple shawl pulled snug against her shoulders in the bookstore's slight chill.

"Hello, dear," she greeted, her eyes crinkling. "Am I too early?"

"Not at all."

"I hope you don't mind, but I brought along a little project." She patted her knitting bag. "Keeps the hands busy while we think things through."

Before Tammy could reply, Olivia reappeared, brushing a stray hair from her face. "I've closed the store, but I'll keep an ear out for the others."

A soft rap at the door announced Wally's arrival. "Ah, the gang's here!" His eyes darted to the exits as he chose a seat—a detail Tammy often included in her character's behavior when in a new place. Life imitating art, or perhaps the other way around?

As they settled in, the conversation ebbed and flowed, so the back door creaking made them all jump. Olivia let out a startled, "Oh goodness!" as Xander stepped inside, balancing a tower of pizza boxes in his lanky arms.

"Xander!" Tammy said. "We're trying to keep a low profile. Won't five pizzas seem suspicious?"

"Nah, I'm a starving teenager. No one batted an eyelid."

The scent of onion and bell peppers filled the room. He placed the boxes on the table. "I bet none of you had lunch because you were too busy researching."

"Do scones count?" asked Mrs. Temperance.

Wally rubbed his stomach. "I didn't realize how late it was."

Tammy's own belly growled in agreement. "Seems like we all forgot to eat." She recalled countless writing sessions where hours flew by unnoticed—a habit that extended to mystery solving.

Xander smirked. "See? I knew you'd need refueling. Dig in." He flipped a lid. The aroma of melted cheese and spices wafted by, making Tammy's mouth water. Xander snagged a slice, strings of mozzarella stretching as he lifted it, and plopped next to Tammy.

Lockie jumped into Tammy's lap, his nose twitching as he sniffed the food. Xander slipped him a piece of pepperoni.

As Tammy reached for a slice, Wally shifted in his seat and cleared his throat. She paused, pizza hovering midair. "What did you find?"

He grinned. "This," he waved a folder around, "is the original case file on Mary Collins's murder. I had to do some fancy talking to get it." He set it on the table. "It's bare bones for a homicide, and more disorganized than a teenager's closet."

Tammy leaned forward, leaving her pizza to cool.

"I've made copies so I can return the originals, but I'm still organizing everything." Wally opened it, revealing a collection of yellow papers, faded photographs, and handwritten notes. "Let's examine the facts. They only ever had one suspect—Victor Walsh, Mary's boyfriend who discovered the body. He was dismissed due to blood spatter patterns, despite a dodgy alibi."

"What was it?" asked Tammy.

"He said he was working in the fields all day, but none of the farmhands could specify the exact time he finished."

"What else have you got?" Xander asked.

Wally picked up a page. "The coroner's report: Single wound to the chest delivered shortly before the body was found at 7:30 p.m."

Tammy swallowed hard, forcing herself to focus on the facts, not the imagery.

"Bruising on the inside of her right arm, consistent with a forceful grab."

Tammy tapped her fingers on the table. "Does that mean the killer was left-handed?"

Olivia's eyes lit up. "Great thought! Let's test it." She stood, tugging at Tammy's arm. "Come on, humor me."

Tammy hesitated, but Olivia's enthusiasm was contagious. She stood, facing her friend. Olivia gripped Tammy's right arm with her left hand, mimicking the pattern indicated in the report.

Olivia grinned. "The pressure points match a left hand."

"Which would narrow our suspect pool," said Tammy.

Xander wiped sauce from his chin. "We need a strong lefty? That doesn't sound hard."

Mrs. Temperance, who had made herself a cup of tea, set down her cup with a gentle clink. "In my day, they used to force left-handed children to write with their right hands. It was considered improper to be a southpaw. Unless you were a pitcher or a boxer."

"Are you suggesting something in particular?" Olivia asked.

"I'm stating a fact, dear."

"The coroner determined the killer was right-handed based on the wound angle," said Wally.

Tammy was grateful Olivia showed no signs of replicating the final blow. "So, we have left-handed bruises, but a right-handed killer?"

Wally nodded. "That could mean two assailants or—"

"Plot twist!" Olivia's eyes widened. "Someone else grabbed Mary before the murder."

"And the murder weapon?" Tammy asked.

Wally laid the evidence list on the table.

Tammy scanned the page. "Only one glass and plate?"

"Mary wasn't expecting company," said Mrs. Temperance, resuming her knitting.

"They found a half-eaten steak but no steak knife," Wally continued.

Xander made a low whistle.

"And they never found it."

Lockie, who had been settled on Tammy's lap, stiffened. His ears twitched and he gave a soft meow.

A missing knife, one place setting, and the contradiction between left-handed bruises and a right-handed killer...

Tammy glanced around at her fellow sleuths, each lost in their own thoughts. The pieces were there, but how did they fit?

Olivia snapped her fingers. "Victor and Mary had an argument earlier that day. And that's why he wasn't at dinner."

"To be a suspect, they need means, motive, and opportunity," said Wally. "Means—"

"I can play this game," said an animated Olivia. "Victor is strong from farm work... and the steak knife was on the table!"

"A crime of opportunity," Mrs. Temperance added.

"Or of passion." Olivia struck a pose, placing a flamboyant hand over her heart. "Motive is a lover's quarrel!"

Everyone was reveling in this 'game' of solving a murder.

Olivia and Xander debated theories, their voices overlapping with enthusiasm. Lockie nudged Tammy's ankle, and she reached down, her fingers sinking into his soft fur. The rhythmic purring grounded her amidst the swirling puzzle pieces.

"There's more to this story than meets the eye," Tammy said.

"That's why it wasn't solved," said Mrs. Temperance.

Impatience gnawed at her, but Olivia placed a reassuring hand on her shoulder. "Did you think we'd crack it on day one? The fun's just beginning."

Tammy sighed, recognizing the truth in Olivia's words. Her characters would never solve the case this early into an investigation.

"What would you have a character in one of your books do next?"

That was the encouragement Tammy needed. "I'd have them dissect the boyfriend's statement."

"There you go."

Tammy turned to Wally. "Let's scrutinize Victor's statement."

Wally shuffled through the folder. "Walsh claims he went to Mary's house to plan a date. Lights were on, but she didn't answer. He looked through the window and saw her on the floor. He kicked in the front door followed by the living-room door, both locked from the inside."

Two locked doors?

"Victor tried to revive Mary, which explains the blood on his clothes when the sheriff arrived." Wally smoothed a wrinkled page. "Here's where it gets interesting. Spatter analysis was only a novel science in '54, and it wouldn't have stood up in court, but they thought it showed Victor wasn't in front of Mary when she was stabbed."

Tammy sucked in her bottom lip. Doubt nagged at her. "I'm not ready to rule him out, despite being cleared back in the day."

"Right. Misinterpretations happen," said Wally.

"They must have asked him questions."

"Walsh was interviewed at the crime scene," Wally began. "It was noted he appeared distressed, with shaking hands and tearful eyes."

"Acting," said Xander with a full mouth.

"Victor confirmed his romantic relationship with Mary, describing her as kind, and claimed no one in town would want to harm her."

Olivia rolled her eyes, making Tammy smile.

"He mentioned Mary seemed distant recently, but thought she was just busy. The officer noted Victor hesitated, suggesting he might be withholding information."

Xander looked up from his laptop. "Maybe she was breaking up with him, and he didn't want to admit it."

"Deputy Mitchell noted Victor struggled to maintain eye contact. While this may stem from trauma, in my experience, it is often a sign of guilt."

Tammy tapped her pen.

"And the...um...*stains* on his clothes?" Xander asked.

*Don't tell me Xander's squeamish.*

"He explained it by saying he tried to see if she was still alive."

"Sounds plausible to me," Tammy said. "If my partner was lying on the floor unresponsive, the last thing I'd be thinking about was disturbing evidence."

Mrs. Temperance paused her knitting. "And what about the shirt itself?"

Wally replied, "Walsh was asked to provide his shirt, and he complied."

"Did they find anything?" asked Xander.

Wally shook his head. "There was no DNA testing back then."

Olivia slumped in her chair. "We can't be sure if it was from trying to help Mary or from killing her."

Mrs. Temperance sighed as she knitted at a steady rhythm. "It's all so circumstantial."

"I know what we need." Olivia disappeared into the bookstore, emerging a few minutes later, pulling a large whiteboard on a sturdy stand.

Mrs. Temperance's jaw dropped. "Where in the store were you hiding that?"

Olivia winked. "This building has all sorts of secrets."

"So, I'm learning."

They spent time mounting articles and notes with magnets. Xander took photos of everything as a digital backup. Olivia started a suspects list with 'VICTOR' in capital letters. Wally stuck a picture of Mary from the file in the middle before drawing a timeline. Mrs. Temperance scribbled important details in elegant cursive.

The once empty frame became a collage of evidence. They stepped back to admire their work. *I can't believe we have an actual murder board.*

# Chapter 11

Tammy bit her lip. "What about the locked room aspect? Last night Lockie went berserk scratching near the living-room's built-in shelves. I combed every inch for hidden mechanisms and spaces but found nothing." Lockie meowed from under the table. "There can't be a secret room or passage there anyway, not with the stove on the other side. I'm stumped."

Lockie meowed again, loud and insistent.

"Maybe there's something you overlooked," said Olivia.

"I'm not sure where else to look..." She turned to Wally. "Did Victor mention anything about it?"

Wally grabbed the file, scanning the pages. "Walsh expressed confusion about how someone committed the murder and vanished without a trace."

"How *did* the killer get out?" asked Mrs. Temperance.

Xander cut in. "They didn't if it was Victor."

Tammy bobbed her head from side to side, weighing the possibility. That made sense.

Olivia bounced her finger against her chin. "Could Victor have broken the door after killing her, *then* placed the keys in the locks?"

Wally considered this. "That would've made it appear as though he was just arriving, adding credibility to his story."

As he spread out photos of the broken doors, his elbow collided with Mrs. Temperance's tea. Photos scattered across the table as he lunged for the tipping cup.

Wally scrambled to gather them, but Tammy snatched one. A paralyzing breath caught in her throat. She fixated on the lifeless body sprawled across a familiar floor. This wasn't one of her fictional crime scenes. This was real. Her core tensed. "Is that...?"

"Yes, dear," Mrs. Temperance confirmed. "That's your living room."

The walls closed in around her. Her friends' discussion became a distant hum. *Someone was murdered in my living room.*

Olivia's arm encircled Tammy's shoulders, solid and reassuring. "It's okay. We're here with you."

Mrs. Temperance's hand enveloped Tammy's. "Deep breaths."

Olivia's voice cut through the panic. "Breathe in—two, three."

Tammy sucked in air, attempting to match Olivia's rhythm.

A deafening bang shattered her attempts.

Tammy's heart leaped.

Olivia yelped.

"Oh fudgsicle!" said Mrs. Temperance. "What on earth was that?"

Olivia faced the back door. "It sounded close."

No one moved. Tammy strained to hear any follow-up sounds—but the silence stretched.

Wally peered out the window. "Nothing out there."

Tammy's body released its defensive posture.

"Probably Caldwell's old rust bucket backfiring," said Xander.

The unexpected noise had broken the tension, allowing Tammy to steady her breathing. Lockie snuggled onto her lap, his rhythmic purring settling her.

"Maybe that's enough for today," Mrs. Temperance suggested. "We can regroup tomorrow."

Exhaustion showed on their faces. They needed rest before diving deeper into the mystery.

Olivia's eyes met Tammy's. "Are you okay to stay in the cottage?"

Tammy hesitated, her gaze drifting to Lockie's as she weighed her options. After a deep breath, "Yes, I'll be fine. I'll...avoid the living room tonight."

Her friends offered words of encouragement, and she accepted Wally's offer of a ride home. How had she come to rely on these new people so quickly?

"Thank you...all." Their selfless gestures touched a long-neglected part of her heart.

*See, Mother, I can make friends.*

# Chapter 12

"Another trail map handed out and an outdoor survival skills book sold," Olivia reported, slipping through the secret door behind Tammy.

Tammy greeted the crew in Olivia's back room. She'd been the last to arrive after a restless night of dreams filled with ghostly dancing steak knives.

She pulled out the letter from the attic. "We haven't talked about this. If it's evidence they didn't have, it might be the key."

She scrutinized the envelope. "It's addressed to someone at my cottage, warning them to keep quiet or else... It's postmarked June. The day and year have faded, but if it's 1954, that would be around the time of Mary's murder."

Wally pressed in. "You think they're connected?"

"It can't be a coincidence," Tammy replied.

Lockie jumped onto the table. He sniffed at the letter and meowed.

Tammy stroked Lockie's back, her fingers sinking into his soft fur. "You can sense things we can't." She gazed into his green eyes, longing to unlock the secrets hidden behind them.

"Okay," Wally said. "The murder happened seventy years ago. That letter paper fits with that era."

"True," Olivia mused, rubbing her temples.

"Let's focus on this new angle," suggested Wally. "It might tell us more about the motive or even introduce another person of interest."

"We need to work out *why* she was being threatened and by *who*," said Mrs. Temperance.

"'If anyone finds out, you'll get it.'" Tammy read aloud. "Does the *recipient* know something about the *sender*? Or does the *sender* know something about the *recipient*?"

"Excellent point, dear," Mrs. Temperance said. "Either way, we've stumbled upon a significant clue."

"Should we hand it over to the sheriff?" asked Xander.

"No," said Wally. "Let's see what we can find first."

Wally flicked through the case file. "Well, well, well." His voice lifted. "They asked Walsh to write his full name and address for the record, noting he wrote with his...*left* hand."

"He made the bruises!" Olivia bolted to the edge of her seat before slumping. "But he can't be the killer."

"Do we have to cross him off our suspect list?" asked Mrs. Temperance. "He's the only one on it."

Xander perked up. "Do we have the handwritten address?"

"Yes." Wally handed it to Xander.

"What if we figured out if the letter was written by a lefty or righty, or matches Victor?" Xander said. "I can research handwriting analysis."

Olivia sat upright. "Brilliant idea."

Tammy turned toward Xander. "How soon will you be ready to make an assessment?"

"I can start now and see what happens." His fingers flew across the keyboard.

"While Xander's working, let's look at Mary," suggested Tammy. "We need every detail we can find to discover motives and suspects?"

Olivia shuffled through her notes. "I searched for her from a genealogy perspective. I found a death certificate. Sometimes, who registered the death provides clues, but it was the coroner."

"More dead ends," said Wally.

"Patience, Wally," retorted Olivia. "She was born in Willowcroft. Her parents left town after subdividing and selling the family farm. They were killed in a car accident not long after. Mary stayed with her grandmother and inherited the cottage when she passed."

"Olivia. Did you get all that via genealogy?"

"Yes, it's amazing what you can find."

Xander gave Olivia a silent clap for her discoveries.

"So, no family," said Tammy. "Wally, did they interview Mary's friends?"

"Yes. Her best friend was Cathy Robinson."

*She'll know Mary's secrets.*

"Cathy confirmed Mary was in a romantic relationship with Walsh. She described him as attentive, bringing Mary flowers and taking her to the movies. She said, and I quote, 'he was very fond of her.'"

Tammy tapped her pen against her notebook. "So, he got the basics right. Any signs of trouble between them? Arguments? Jealousy?"

Wally shook his head. "When questioned about potential tensions or disagreements, Cathy stated she hadn't noticed any issues, describing the couple as 'happy.'"

A scoff almost escaped Tammy. The old "perfect couple" story.

Wally skimmed the report before continuing. "Cathy didn't mention anyone she thought might harm Mary, saying she was 'well-liked by everyone in town.'"

Olivia rolled her eyes, leaning back in her chair. "Don't people always say that? Just once, I'd like to hear someone say something bad about a dead person."

"Olivia!" said Mrs. Temperance, her knitting needles pausing mid stitch.

She shrugged. "I only mean if it's true."

Olivia had said what Tammy had been thinking. "I agree." Her words came out stronger than intended. "Everyone says the deceased was the kindest person ever known and loved by all. But let's be honest—that's rarely the whole truth, is it?"

Mrs. Temperance tsked. "When did you girls become so jaded?"

Tammy tried to keep a neutral expression. *I'm being real.*

"They considered the robbery angle," Wally said, "but Cathy implied there was nothing of value to steal, stating Mary lived 'simply.'" He paused, stroking his chin. "The officer noted that while Cathy was forthcoming, she seemed hesitant or uncertain at times, with pauses in her responses."

Was Cathy nervous?

Olivia piped in, "Was she hiding trouble in paradise? That Victor's motive was...a lover's tiff?"

Tammy snorted at Olivia's phrasing. "Lover's tiff?" She shook her head, amused. "I feel like we're in an Agatha Christie novel."

"Well, my dear," Olivia quipped, adopting an exaggerated British accent, "anyone is capable of dastardly deeds." She chuckled at her own joke, and laughter bubbled around the room.

"That's especially true if there was someone else at play," Tammy said.

*Ooh, a secret lover? For him or her?* Tammy tried to picture Mary's life, shrouded in suspicion and secrets. What pressures had the young woman faced? What desperate choices might she have made? Was she betrayed or the betrayer?

# Chapter 13

"Did you find anything useful at the library yesterday?" Olivia directed at Tammy, who was deep in thought.

"Lockie was with me, of course." Tammy glanced at him, curled up beside her. Lockie twitched an ear. "The librarian didn't seem too thrilled about it."

"Maxine's more of a dog person," said Mrs. Temperance.

*Maxine? I'd pegged her as something more severe, like Virginia, to match the glasses and perpetual frown.*

A smirk crossed her lips as she remembered Maxine's reaction. The woman scowled, her pinched nose wrinkling further. "Absolutely no animals!"

"Lockie gave her one of those mysterious looks of his, and somehow...she backed off." Tammy shook her head. "I swear, this cat has some sort of special power."

"But did you find anything, dear?" asked Mrs. Temperance.

"I discovered there were *two* newspapers back in the fifties. I had searched the Willowcroft *Gazette*, but the Willowcroft *Tribune* also circulated in 1954. When it closed, their archives were put onto microfilm and donated to the library."

"I remember the *Tribune*," said Mrs. Temperance. "They often covered stories the *Gazette* wouldn't touch."

Tammy handed documents to Xander to add to their digital file. "I scrolled through the records forward in time from the murder. Most of it was typical small-town news—the new water tower, school events, prize-winning squashes.

But I found one article of interest. It was brief—the sheriff's department wasn't releasing details and reporters were struggling for information."

"Sounds like they had nothing *to* share," Wally interrupted. "Better to be tight-lipped than admit you've got zip."

"But one journalist camped out at the diner across from the department, noting everyone who went in and out. I compiled a list of names we can cross reference with the witness statements and see if we find any new leads."

Wally arranged his file. "Let's take a gander."

Chewing her lip, Tammy said, "Carol Martin."

Wally rifled through the papers. "'I saw a fella with a gun in his hand, but I figure it's best not get involved. Mindin' your own business is the way to go in this town.'"

Olivia flopped in her chair. "But Mary was stabbed, not shot."

"Could be an unrelated incident," Tammy said.

"Or maybe someone trying to throw off the investigation," Xander added.

"Seems like a dead end to me," Wally grumbled. "Who's next?"

"Reginald McLeod," Tammy said, noting a subtle shift in Mrs. Temperance's posture. Her knitting needles paused.

Olivia bounced in her chair.

"The McLeod family bought part of the Collins' farm. His property bordered the cottage."

Olivia flipped through her notepad. "Mary's parents sold the farm to the McLeods in 1946."

"Let's see what Reginald had to say," Wally said, finding the statement.

Mrs. Temperance shifted in her seat. "I—"

Wally plowed ahead, morphing into a gruff, rural accent. "I was fast asleep when I was woken by my sheep making a ruckus. When I turned the outside light on, they were running around all manic like, as though they had been spooked."

Tammy's brow furrowed. "Spooked? By what?"

The killer? Or—

Mrs. Temperance's annoyed huff snapped Tammy out of her thoughts. "If I may add, I learned something rather interesting at the nursing home about Reginald McLeod. Mr. Hill mentioned overhearing a heated argument outside the little blue cottage about the land sale."

A cold breeze swept through Tammy. "My cottage?"

"The very same."

She thought of the strange man in the old coat, the mysterious disappearing flowers from her garden.

"Tempers flared, voices raised—" Mrs. Temperance continued, "that kind of passion may lead to—"

"Murder," Wally finished her sentence.

"Do we have a new suspect?" Tammy asked. Is this the break they needed?

Olivia pushed her glasses up the bridge of her nose. "I'll add him to our suspects list."

"Let's think this through," Wally said, his hands rearranging the papers in front of him. "What would be the motive? Greed? Revenge?"

"Maybe the sale didn't go as planned," Tammy suggested, her brain firing through multiple octaves. "Or perhaps there was a disagreement over property lines or access rights?"

"Land disputes can get ugly," Wally acknowledged.

Olivia's face sparkled. "This is sounding like a classic family feud. The Collinses and the McLeods, entangled by a farm."

"People who feel cheated," Wally said, "can hold a grudge for years."

Olivia snapped her fingers. "Exactly! Like in the movie *Arsenic and Old Lace*, where the murders were rooted in an old family feud. Though hopefully with less elderberry wine involved." She chuckled at her own reference, but Tammy was too preoccupied to join in.

"Or what if," Tammy said, her mind racing, "the land was worth more than anyone realized? Maybe there was something valuable on the property only a few people knew about."

Mrs. Temperance's knitting needles clacked rhythmically as she added, "Oil, perhaps? Or gold? Wouldn't that be something!"

Tammy's thoughts drifted to the strange man lurking around her cottage. Was he a McLeod? The uneasy feeling in her stomach intensified with the nagging worry they might trigger something dangerous. How far would someone go to protect their secrets?

Mrs. Temperance's needles halted. "I have an idea." Her eyes twinkled with mischief. "I'll call an emergency knitting circle meeting."

Tammy blinked, confused. "A knitting circle? How would that help?"

Mrs. Temperance leaned in, her shawl slipping off one shoulder. "My dear, you'd be surprised by those ladies. If anyone knows about a feud over the Collins farm, or has dirt on Reginald, it'll be them."

Olivia appeared skeptical. "What constitutes an emergency? I mean, we can't broadcast that we're investigating a decades-old murder."

"Oh, don't worry. I'll tell them the hospital called, saying they need more blankets for the babies. Works every time."

"Ah," Olivia responded, as a wry smile curled her lips. "Nothing mobilizes the troops quite like the prospect of helping babies."

Tammy chuckled at the clever subterfuge, contemplating the wealth of information the knitting circle might possess. A treasure trove of local lore and long-held secrets just waiting to be divulged. "Who knew knitting could be so...covert?"

"You're a devious mastermind, Mrs. Temperance," Olivia said, shaking her head. "I love it."

Mrs. Temperance resumed her knitting with renewed vigor, wearing a self-satisfied smirk.

Olivia drew everyone's attention. "Let's add the motive of 'land dispute' under Reginald's name." She scribbled on their murder board.

Unease had built during the conversation as a nagging idea formed. Did the McLeods still covet the land? Her land?

*Do I tell them? What if they think I'm imagining things? Or worse—what if I'm right, and it's connected?* Tammy forced a swallow. "There's something I need to tell you."

All eyes snapped to her. A flush crept up her neck.

"Has anyone noticed anything...unusual recently?" Blank expressions greeted her as she scanned the group. "I might have someone to add to our list."

The air thickened with tension. "The suspicious man from my garden."

Mrs. Temperance's needles stilled, the soothing ticking that had been a constant backdrop now absent. "What man?" Her eyes were sharp with interest.

Tammy took a deep breath, her gaze dropping to the table. *I barely understand what happened myself. But if it's related and I don't say anything... It's time to find out if I trusted the right people.* She exhaled. "Well, it's a strange story. I've had a couple of...encounters, I guess you'd call them."

As she recounted the incidents—the shadowy figure fleeing her property, leaving a trail of plant material, and the mysterious disappearance of flowers from her garden—the expressions of her newfound friends shifted from curiosity to concern.

"All your lovely flowers gone?" Mrs. Temperance asked in genuine dismay.

Tammy shrugged, trying to mask her own disappointment with nonchalance. "Well, I didn't plant them, and if I'm being honest, I'm not sure how long they would have lasted under my care. But yes, they are all gone."

A heaviness fell to the pit of her stomach. Had her arrival in Willowcroft stirred up more than old memories? Was this decades-old murder now personal? "I wasn't sure what to think at first, but now..."

"Let's add this mysterious garden intruder to our list of things to investigate," Olivia decided, reaching for a whiteboard marker.

Mrs. Temperance was deep in thought. "Were all the elderflowers taken?"

"Uh, maybe." Tammy squinted her eyes as she tried to recall the exact state of her garden. "But I'm not sure if that was all they took."

"Was he wearing an old coat?"

"Yes! So strange for summer."

"Old Lawrence," Mrs. Temperance said with certainty, resuming her knitting.

"Who?" Tammy asked, her writer's mind already conjuring images of a mysterious, grizzled old man.

Olivia's eyes lit up. "Lawrence? The recluse who lives past the woods?"

"Yes, that's him. He's been living off the land around here for years. He's known for his elderberry syrup."

Tammy's forehead wrinkled. "What does that have to do with my missing flowers?"

"Elderflowers are a key ingredient in elderberry syrup," said Mrs. Temperance. "They need to be picked early in the morning before the heat of the day, to preserve their delicate flavor."

Tammy's eyes widened. "So, he was picking flowers for his syrup?"

The idea someone might have been pilfering her garden for commercial gain was bizarre, yet oddly mundane.

Mrs. Temperance nodded. "Yes, he likely didn't think anyone would mind, given the cottage had been unoccupied. He might have even been cultivating the plants to increase his crop."

Tammy's eyebrows shot up. "He planted them himself?"

"Possibly. Lawrence is peculiar but harmless. He's probably unaware of how this might have upset you." Mrs. Temperance sat forward. "If the elderflowers are all gone, he's unlikely to come back. I don't think we need to put him on any list except the one that includes all the quirky people in town."

Tammy exhaled, her shoulders dropping as the tension eased from her body. She hadn't realized how tense she'd been about the mysterious garden intruder. "That's...actually comforting," she admitted.

Olivia rubbed "garden man" off the board.

"Peggy serves his elderberry syrup in the diner," said Mrs. Temperance. "Next time you're there, you should try it—it's divine."

Olivia chuckled. "You should ask for a discount, seeing as you supplied the raw ingredients."

Tammy chewed her lower lip, lost.

"You good there, Tammy?" Wally's concerned tone broke through her reverie. "You look a million miles away."

Tammy blinked, focusing back on the group. "I was just thinking… if Lawrence isn't linked to the case, he can't help us." She ran a hand through her hair.

*Am I cut out for this? Inventing secrets in fiction is one thing, but this is different.*

Mrs. Temperance's needles clicked. "We'll get to the bottom of this yet. Sometimes the answers come from the most unexpected places. Olivia's comparison to *Arsenic and Old Lace*, and her referencing elderberry wine as the murder weapon, made me think of Lawrence."

Olivia beamed with pride.

"However," Mrs. Temperance continued, "the movie was less about a family feud and more about…well, something else entirely."

Olivia's joy crumbled.

"Just another colorful quirk of Willowcroft," said Xander.

"Colorful is one word for it," Wally said with a chuckle. "This town has more characters than a soap opera."

"And every character has a story." Olivia's mojo had returned. "We need the one tied to Mary."

Stories. Tammy's writer's heart latched onto the word. She glanced at her hands, imagining them typing out the narrative they were living. This is real life with real consequences. Did she have what it took to find the ending? She hadn't seen her own ending coming.

The theft of her manuscript—the best novel she'd ever written—had ended her time in the traditional publishing sphere. Not to mention the extra dent in her professional pride—what kind of mystery writer couldn't figure out how her own masterpiece had vanished from her apartment?

Dom had discouraged her from looking into it too closely. At the time, she'd thought it was to spare her disappointment. But now? There had been something almost calculated in his insistence, something she'd ignored in her desperation to hold on to the one good thing she had.

Wally steered the conversation to Xander who was hunched over his laptop. "How are you doing with the handwriting analysis?"

Xander spread out Victor's statement and the attic letter. "We wanted to know if Victor wrote the threat. I scanned our two samples into the computer to zoom in on the finer details." He swiveled the laptop so everyone could see the images side by side in a large format.

A jolt of unease ran through Tammy. The words leaped off the screen at her, now a more potent message than when she'd first discovered it.

"I compared the two pieces. Victor's writing slants slightly to the left, consistent with a left-hander. The letter, however, slants to the right—indicative of a right-hander."

"So, Victor likely didn't write the letter," Tammy concluded.

"That seems to be the case," Xander confirmed. "There were also obvious stylistic differences between the two samples, making it clear they weren't written by the same person."

"Well done, Xander," Wally said, taking charge once more.

"Time to cross him off the list for good?" Olivia clarified as she approached the board.

Mrs. Temperance checked her watch. "Oh. I have phone calls to make. Time to rally the Willow-Crafters."

# Chapter 14

Cinnamon and steeping tea filled the air.

"Betty, dear, pass me the teapot, please," said Hazel.

Betty, sorting through skeins of soft yarn, looked up. "Of course. Your cinnamon rolls smell delightful as always."

Marjorie Hubbard's slim frame stiffened. "I do hope you've used less sugar this time. It's not proper for ladies our age to indulge so recklessly."

Hazel bit back a chuckle, remembering Marjorie's penchant for strictness from her days running the town grocery. "I assure you, Marjorie, these are perfectly sensible cinnamon rolls."

As she arranged the teacups, Hazel pondered how to steer the conversation to the Collins farm without arousing suspicion.

Beatrice leaned in. "Did you hear about young Lane Jakeman? Caught stealing apples from Parkland's orchard again."

Marjorie tutted. "In my day, children respected their elders and their neighbors' property."

Hazel saw her chance. "Speaking of property, I was thinking about the old Collins farm."

Betty's needles paused mid-stitch. "Why is it called the Collins farm if the McLeods own it?"

"The McLeods bought the farm from the Collins family," said Hazel. "I wondered if there was an issue with the sale? Perhaps a dispute over the boundaries?"

She saw the gears turning in Marjorie's head, the woman's posture rigid with recollection. "The little blue cottage wasn't included in the sale, if that's what you mean. It is surrounded by the McLeod farm."

Hazel feigned surprise, her wrinkled hands clasping together. "Who has owned the cottage all these years?"

Marjorie straightened her conservative dress. "If I'm not mistaken, the council has owned that bit of land for some time. It's had a spotty tenant history, as you know."

*The council?* Why would they hold on to such a small parcel of land?

She poured tea with a steady hand. "How interesting. I do love local history. More tea, anyone?"

Betty proffered her cup.

Hazel kept her tone innocent and curious. "Did the cottage cause some sort of feud?"

"But there's no Collins family in town to feud with, so it's not an issue," said Marjorie.

Hazel appraised the faces around her for any flicker of emotion, any sign of further knowledge being unspoken.

"True," she replied, "but sometimes, such disputes fester and spread."

"My, these blankets are coming along nicely," Betty changed the subject, lifting her work for inspection. "The babies will be so cozy wrapped in these."

Hazel bit back a sigh of frustration. She needed to find the right thread to pull.

Marjorie tilted her head. "Why the sudden interest in ancient history?" she asked, with a hint of suspicion.

A nervous laugh bubbled as she patted her bun. "Oh, you know me. Always learning. It keeps the mind sharp."

Marjorie pursed her lips, clearly unconvinced. "Well, there's no harm in speculating," she conceded. "If there was a dispute, it may have been about access rights. The cottage and its land were part of the original Collins farm."

Did Reginald feel entitled to that land? Did he resent Mary for living there?

She stared at her half-finished blanket, the pastel colors blurring. Why hadn't Reginald bought the cottage after Mary's death if he'd killed her for it? The lack of a clear motive nagged at Hazel. Her instincts told her they could strike him off the suspects list. Were they back to square one?

"Ladies," Hazel said, "I appreciate your insights. You've given me much to ponder... Now, shall we focus on finishing these blankets? Those little ones at the hospital need our warmth."

# Chapter 15

The crackle of static from Mrs. Temperance's ancient flip phone pierced the quiet of Olivia's back room. Tammy winced. The tinny voice of Marjorie Hubbard filled the air, her words tumbling out in a breathless rush and audible to everyone in the room.

"Hazel, you won't believe what just happened! I was talking with Katie and a customer at Mrs. Hubbard's Cupboard about the emergency knitting circle. We were discussing the little blue cottage when suddenly we heard a crash. We turned to see a jar shattered on the floor and this hooligan in a T-shirt with some kind of ghost on it dashing toward us. He was in such a hurry, he nearly bowled me over! It was the strangest thing—everything was calm until we mentioned the Collins farm, and then chaos!"

Something nagged at the edges of Tammy's memory, like a word stuck on the tip of her tongue. A ghost T-shirt. The image of the young man from a few days ago floated up—that distinctive flash of yellow on blue she'd glimpsed. Her gut screamed that these details mattered, even as her conscious mind didn't quite grasp why. The connection was there, hovering just out of reach.

She exchanged a glance with Xander, who mouthed, "Drama queen," making Olivia giggle. Should she mention her T-shirt-wearing man? No, that was too far-fetched. The coat-wearing man turned out to be nothing.

Olivia rolled her eyes. "Why won't Mrs. Hubbard admit she's a gossip?"

"Of course, Marjorie," said Mrs. Temperance, giving Olivia the side-eye, "we appreciate your...discretion. Was he stealing?"

"We're not sure," Marjorie admitted, indignation clear. "But what are our youth coming to today?"

Wally shook his head. "Classic Marjorie."

Mrs. Temperance thanked her and hung up, turning to the others. "I'm not sure what all this means... Tammy, who did you purchase the little blue cottage from?"

Tammy blinked, caught off guard. "Um, some trust, I think." She fumbled for her phone, pulled up the contract, and squinted at the small text. "The Willowcroft Trust."

Why was Mrs. Temperance asking about this now? Did it have something to do with Marjorie's call? She glanced at Lockie, coiled up in a warm spot, envying the cat's apparent nonchalance.

"The Willowcroft Trust." Mrs. Temperance's eyes sparkled with the joy of a new revelation. "Well, if the town owned that land, Reginald McLeod could have purchased it at any time, right?"

Tammy's breath caught. She hadn't considered that angle. Her gaze darted to Olivia who was absently twirling a strand of her auburn hair in deep concentration.

"That's...that's true," Tammy said, trying to understand the implications. "So, why wouldn't he have bought it before now?"

"Because it didn't matter, and certainly not worth killing someone over," said Mrs. Temperance.

"Do we rule him out as a suspect?" Olivia asked.

"My gut says yes, dear. I'd be crossing him off the list in my notebook—if I hadn't misplaced it."

"I'm sure it will turn up." Olivia adjusted her glasses. "I've dug through every record, but there's no will."

Tammy imagined herself at twenty-five, living alone in a quaint cottage. Would she have thought to make a will? The idea seemed so...final. So, no.

Olivia shook her head. "And honestly, why would she? No husband, no kids, no other relatives we know of."

No will, and no family. "So, who inherited the cottage?"

"The property reverted to the town council," Mrs. Temperance said. "A.k.a., the Willowcroft Trust."

Tammy glanced at the others, noting their rapt expressions. "The town owned it? Until..."

"Until you bought it," Mrs. Temperance finished, a hint of a smile playing on her wrinkled features.

"So, there's no McLeod descendant coming after his inheritance." Which means that wasn't the reason for the young man with a yellow logo on his T-shirt lurking around her cottage.

Olivia stood, heading to the murder board. "Goodbye, Reginald."

Tammy rested her elbows on the table. The wooden chair creaked beneath her. "If McLeod isn't guilty, we need to revisit his statement. If he'd killed Mary, it would be full of lies. If he didn't, he's the closest neighbor."

Mrs. Temperance hummed in agreement. "Read his full statement, Wally."

Wally pulled out Reginald's statement. "He talks about his sheep being spooked after he'd gone to bed."

"Someone running from the cottage may have crossed his field, disturbing the sheep," said Olivia.

Wally scrutinized the page.

"There's a faint handwritten note. It says 'Reginald is known for turning in before dusk, often as early as five or six in the evening. Thus, rendering his information unreliable in determining a time.'"

Tammy glanced at the timeline. "Victor found Mary's body at seven-thirty?" She stood and paced. "If Reginald's sheep were spooked after then, it might correlate with the killer's escape."

"No specifics given?" asked Olivia.

Wally skimmed the statement. "No, but he turned on the outside light so it must have been after dark."

Xander's fingers sped up on his laptop. "Sunset that night was nine-thirteen p.m. We're looking at a time after that."

"That's way after Victor found the body," Mrs. Temperance pointed out.

"Wouldn't the killer have already fled?" asked Olivia.

"Unless they were hiding nearby," Wally suggested. "Perhaps they stayed hidden until later to avoid detection."

Olivia snapped her fingers. "Maybe Victor interrupted the killer, who hid until the sheriff left, escaping through Reg's field and disturbing the sheep."

"A compelling theory," Mrs. Temperance agreed, "and explains the locked room mystery."

Tammy stopped pacing and faced the group. "But I haven't found a hiding place in the cottage," Tammy pointed out. "There has to be another explanation."

Wally reclined in his chair, a glimmer of admiration in his eyes. "I have to hand it to you all. You're seeing correlations the original investigators missed."

Mrs. Temperance nodded. "What other names do we have on that list, Tammy? Perhaps we can find more overlooked details."

Tammy read from her *Tribune* list. "Eleanor Cross."

The room was filled with the sound of shuffling paper as Wally flipped and re-flipped the pages with pursed lips. "I can't find anything on Eleanor Cross."

"A clerical error?" Olivia scribbled the name with a question mark before stepping back to survey the board.

Xander tapped away on his laptop in the corner.

"Next on the list is a *Max* Cross."

"Sorry, definitely no one with the surname of Cross is in these files," said Wally without looking.

Olivia added Max Cross's name also with a question mark. "We can work on the Crosses later."

Tammy slid her finger down the list. "Try Donald Turner."

Wally located Donald's statement with a triumphant grunt. "Here we go. 'I saw Abigail walking along Cedar Lane that evening, but I'm certain she wouldn't have done it. She was busy knitting a sweater for her grandson. A person with a heart of gold like her couldn't possibly commit such a crime!'"

Olivia's hands mimicked the motions of knitting needles as she rolled her eyes. "Are we supposed to believe someone is innocent just because they're knitting a sweater?" She turned to Mrs. Temperance. "You're safe."

Mrs. Temperance clucked her tongue.

Tammy raised an eyebrow. "Sounds like Donald had a crush on Abigail if you ask me."

"It doesn't help us right now," Xander said without removing his eyes from his laptop. The tapping of the keys remaining in a steady rhythm.

Lockie padded across the table, weaving between piles of papers.

"Let's continue with Margaret Wagner," said Tammy.

"She said, 'I didn't see anything, but I heard Mrs. Reynold's cat meowing loudly. It was definitely up to something sinister.'"

"The cat did it!" Olivia exclaimed with a laugh. The tension in the room dissipated as they shared a chuckle. Lockie flicked his tail, as if he, too, understood the joke.

"Not much happens in our little town," said Mrs. Temperance. "A loud cat was probably the most excitement poor Margaret had seen in some time."

The comment reminded Tammy this sleepy community was not accustomed to such violence.

As they continued through the list, it became obvious none of the witnesses had seen anything helpful. Wally shook his head as he closed the file. "It's easy to see why the case remains unsolved. The sheriff had nothing to work with. They didn't stand a chance."

A contemplative silence settled over the group. The only sound was the hum of Xander's laptop.

Tammy peered at their board. "Who are Eleanor and Max Cross?"

"Good question," Wally replied, flipping through the file once more. "There is no statement from either of them."

"Could they have been there for another matter?" Olivia suggested.

Xander's fingers flew across the keyboard of his laptop. "Maybe they were there about the bank heist."

# Chapter 16

"Bank heist! What bank heist?" Tammy's mind spun. *What in the world was Xander going on about? It sounded like a plot twist from one of her books.*

Xander looked up from his screen and adjusted his glasses. "Yeah, three weeks before the murder, there was a headline about a bank heist. It's unsolved, too." How could he drop a bombshell like that so casually?

"Two major unsolved crimes within weeks…" Tammy said, as her stomach churned. *I don't even know if I can solve one crime, let alone two.*

"I don't believe in coincidences," said Wally.

"Tell us more, Xander dear," Mrs. Temperance urged.

"Tammy searched forward in time from the murder, so I thought I'd go back in time. I made it to January 1952. There wasn't much about the little blue cottage apart from garden awards, fireplace renovation notices for extra workers, and other unhelpful social news. But three weeks before the murder, I couldn't resist the headline even if it didn't mention the cottage or Mary."

"How scrumptious! A bank heist is totally something from a Hollywood movie," said Olivia as she bounced in her chair. "Tell us more."

Olivia's enthusiasm radiated into the room like a lighthouse beacon, cutting through Tammy's fog of doubt. *Why can't I enjoy the process like she can?* Tammy attempted to smother the nagging insecurities threatening to consume her. This wasn't the moment for second-guessing; the pivotal revelation demanded her full attention. She steeled herself, determined to focus on every word.

"From what I can find online, the Willowcroft bank was broken into in the dead of night," Xander explained. "They entered the vault and got away with a significant amount of cash."

"Why is this the first we're hearing of it?" Tammy asked.

Xander shrugged. "Different case, different file. The records aren't linked."

"I wonder if they should be," said Tammy. Was the heist a time wasting distraction or a critical clue?

Mrs. Temperance huffed. "Two major crimes, barely a month apart, and no arrests made? What was the sheriff doing?"

"It doesn't reflect well," Olivia said. "But we can't assume Eleanor and Max's visit is related to either the robbery or murder." She turned to Xander. "Nice work thinking outside the box, though."

Xander sprouted a grin.

*See how easy it is to give praise, Mother? Don't go there, Tammy. Focus.* "Let's research the Crosses and see where that takes us."

"Agreed," said Olivia. "There has to be a reason they were there that week."

Wally held up a hand. "Not everyone who walks into the building is a suspect or a witness."

"Maybe they were selling Girl Scout cookies," joked Xander.

"Or Nick Bradley's grandfather upended their trash cans." Olivia giggled.

Wally gave Xander and Olivia the side-eye. "If they were there for something other than giving a statement about the murder, it wouldn't get a mention in our murder file."

"The journalist staking out the station wouldn't know why people were there," offered Tammy. "They were noting everyone who walked into the station from their vantage point as they had nothing else to follow up."

"Who knows what it means or how thoroughly they investigated back then," Olivia said.

"Two major crimes? That's gotta be overwhelming, right?" said Xander.

"More like sloppy work," Wally grumbled. "We won't make the same mistakes. Let's learn more about the Crosses, and dig deeper into *both* cases."

"I'll head back to the library in the morning," Tammy said.

"Guys," Xander interrupted, ogling his laptop with a mixture of surprise and triumph. "I've found Eleanor Cross's statement."

"Really?" *Are we about to have a breakthrough?* Even Lockie perked his ears.

"Let me see," Wally insisted, as everyone crowded around Xander's screen.

"I stumbled upon a digital version of the original file. I didn't wanna say anything until I was sure I could crack it—"

Wally held up a hand as he turned his head away from Xander. "Don't tell me how you got it. I don't want the details."

Who cares how he got it? "What did it say?" Tammy asked.

"She was walking her dog before going to bed on the night of the murder. She saw a short figure running away from the cottage. They were too far away to make out clearly, but when asked if male or female, she said they were wearing pants."

Olivia's eyes brightened. "In the 1950s, not many women wore pants, suggesting a man. Although it would be a good disguise for a woman back then."

Wally nodded slowly. "This is big. Eleanor Cross gave a description of someone at the scene. Someone short enough to be a woman but assumed to be a man because they wore pants."

Xander snapped his laptop shut. "Still no statement from Max, but we've got a lead."

The investigation was finally moving ahead.

Tammy ran her hand through her hair. "But why was her statement missing from the original file?"

"Perhaps it was misplaced," Mrs. Temperance suggested. "Wally did say it was quite disorganized."

Wally rubbed his chin, avoiding eye contact. "Yeah, feels like it's been dropped on the floor a time or two and scooped back up. Happens sometimes."

"So, Eleanor's statement is lying under an old filing cabinet, never to be seen again," said Olivia.

Mrs. Temperance looked at Xander. "Thankfully, it was digitized."

"We were lucky," said Xander. "Not all the case files are available. They were given a grant to digitize, but the money ran out before they were finished."

"Regardless of how or why it was missing, we can't ignore this lead," Wally declared. "We need to find out more about Eleanor Cross and what she saw that night."

"Agreed," Olivia affirmed, her eyes meeting Wally's. "Earlier we decided the killer could still be alive—so Eleanor could be, too."

"She may remember more details if we can jog her memory," said Tammy.

"I can't recall a Cross family in town," said Mrs. Temperance, "but one of the Willow-Crafters might."

Lockie let out a low, guttural growl directed at the back door. The tension in the room rose as the group exchanged quick glances.

A shiver coursed through Tammy.

Olivia stood. "Maybe our meeting has stirred up some interest." She peeked out the back window. "False alarm. But it's getting late. Let's wrap up for today."

Heads nodded around the table. Tammy stroked Lockie, trying to soothe the agitated cat and her own nerves.

Xander said, "Shall we meet in the morning to work out our next steps?"

"Absolutely," Wally said. "I'll bring pastries from Sweet Crumbs for everyone."

The group agreed and prepared to leave.

Mrs. Temperance wrapped her purple shawl around her as she approached the front door. "Until tomorrow, my dears. Keep your wits about you."

"I'll walk you across the square, Mrs. Temperance," Wally said, as he offered her an arm, which she accepted. He tipped his hat to Olivia. Such a gentleman.

Xander tucked his laptop into his backpack. "See you for breakfast."

Tammy scooped up Lockie. He nuzzled against her chin. She bid Olivia good-night before the store door was locked behind her. What a day. Revelations and resolutions, twists, and turns. If only she could conjure evidence like in her writing. Finding clues in real life was a lot harder. *I'm not listening to you, Mother. I can do this. We can do this.*

# Chapter 17

Olivia stood in front of the murder board. She marinated in the photos, documents, and multicolored sticky notes. The smell of brewing coffee filled the back room. This was so much more delectable than any mystery novel or any family tree she'd untangled.

The display before her was tangible evidence of an unsolved crime in Willowcroft. Who would have thought her bookstore would become the headquarters for a real-life investigation? *I love having alone time with the board.* That was only possible because the team had chosen her back room as their unofficial home.

She adjusted her glasses, leaning in to examine the photo of the key in the door. Was it a clever ruse? Or had Mary locked herself in, only to meet a grisly fate?

A smile played at the corners of her mouth as she thought about Tammy moving to town. She had known, somehow, the mystery writer would bring intrigue and adventure to their sleepy community. But this? This was beyond her wildest dreams. A decades-old unsolved murder, a bank heist, cryptic letters, and missing witness statements. It was like something straight out of an Agatha Christie novel, but unfolding right before her eyes.

The bell above the store door tinkled, signaling the arrival of her fellow amateur sleuths. Olivia's stomach flipped. What new leads would they uncover today? What secrets would they bring to light?

She took one last glimpse at the board, drinking in the details. This was it—the adventure she'd been waiting for her whole life. And she was determined to see it through to the end, no matter where the clues might lead them.

Tammy entered, cradling Lockie. "Morning, Olivia." She set Lockie down, and the feline sauntered over to a patch of sunlight streaming through the back window and wrapped himself into a cozy ball.

"Good morning," Olivia said, gesturing to the steaming pot on the counter. "Coffee's ready if you need a pick-me-up."

Tammy poured herself a cup.

The bell chimed again, and Wally strode in, a large box balanced in his arms. The scent of fresh pastries wafted through the air, mingling with the coffee.

"Ladies," he greeted, setting the box on the table. "I've brought sustenance from Sweet Crumbs." He lifted the lid to reveal an assortment of flaky croissants, muffins, and fruit-filled Danishes.

"Wally, you're a saint," Olivia declared, reaching for a chocolate croissant.

He shrugged. "Can't solve murders on an empty belly."

Xander arrived next. The lanky teenager shuffled in, his ever-present laptop tucked under one arm. Dark circles rimmed his eyes. "Late night?" Olivia asked. She could relate to the signs of sleep deprivation—how many times had she worked deep into the night poring over genealogy records?

"Hey, guys," Xander mumbled, making a beeline for the coffeepot. He gulped coffee as he nodded.

"Not too much caffeine for you, Xander. You're still a growing teenager," Olivia teased.

The final jangle of the bell announced Mrs. Temperance's arrival. She swept into the room, resplendent in a vibrant rainbow shawl. Her knitting bag, bulging with yarn and needles, swung from her arm. "Good morning."

Mrs. Temperance settled into a new comfortable chair and pulled out her needles. The commotion roused Lockie, who padded over to join them.

Olivia grinned at the assembled group. "Shall we get started? We've got a murder to solve." She turned to Xander. "Did you find any other discrepancies between the file versions?"

"Well, I digitized the hard copy to make cross-referencing easier...Eleanor Cross's statement was the only difference—"

"Well, that's a relief," said Wally.

"I am curious, Wally, how *did* you get the file?" Olivia asked.

"I used up a favor to get me in the archives for five minutes."

Xander scoffed at Wally's answer. "How is that any different from me hacking into the online version?"

Wally shifted in his chair and averted his eyes. His hands played with the already neat folder. "Still no mention of Max?" he asked, steering the conversation elsewhere.

Was he dodging Xander's question on purpose? Xander had a point. But could Wally ever come to terms with the more modern methods?

Tammy interrupted Olivia's thoughts, "Maybe Max was escorting his wife to make her statement."

"Interesting," said Olivia, her attention drawn to Mrs. Temperance, who was quietly knitting in the armchair Olivia had brought from upstairs. "How do you like your chair, Mrs. Temperance?"

"It's perfect. Thank you for thinking of me. It's easier to knit here than at the table. My mind works best when my needles are clicking."

Tammy steered the conversation back to the case. "We need to find out more about Eleanor Cross. Do we know anything apart from her owning a dog which she was walking that night?" she asked, shifting her gaze around the group.

Xander scanned the files before answering. "The log says, 'young Eleanor Cross presented.'" His eyes met Tammy's. "That's all we've got."

"Hopefully," said Olivia, "Max was her father rather than her husband."

Tammy leaped up, almost upending her chair and startling the group. "High school yearbooks! If Eleanor Cross was young enough to be in school and went to Willowcroft High, there's a chance the library might have her yearbooks. It could give us more information about her and even a photo."

"Great idea!" Olivia agreed, matching Tammy's enthusiasm. "A picture might jog some memories for those who have lived here longer."

"I'll check," Xander said. His fingers danced across the keyboard. "Here we go! Yep, they have yearbooks going back as far as 1925!"

"Excellent work, Xander," said Mrs. Temperance.

Xander gave a mock seated bow, eliciting a chuckle.

"I'm already up," said Tammy. "I'll dash there now. It won't take long. It's such a novelty how close everything is compared to LA." Lockie fell into step beside her.

The library smelled of wood polish, which tickled Tammy's nose and made Lockie sneeze. "Shush. If you're discovered, she'll kick you out." He sauntered on as if to say, 'she wouldn't dare.'

Tammy followed, hoping they wouldn't be noticed.

She found the 1954 Willowcroft High School yearbook and slid it from the shelf. The hard cover creaked. Tammy flipped through the black-and-white photos, transporting herself back to a simpler time. She admired the hairstyles and outfits.

Finally, Tammy saw a caption that read: Eleanor Cross. The above picture showed a girl with a shy smile, kind eyes, and short, dark hair. Tammy studied the girl's face. What secrets did she hold from that fateful night? She continued flicking through the book. No other Crosses. But she stumbled upon a candid photo of Eleanor with a dapper young man, his arm around her shoulders. Eleanor's face sparkled. "Eleanor and Tom—Willowcroft High's sweethearts!"

After reminiscing about young love for a moment, and cursing her latest love, she used her phone to take copies of both photos. Every new piece of information was gripping. Now she knew what her characters experienced as they discovered clues. Where would Eleanor's story take them next?

Olivia was deep in her genealogy mindset when the store's front door bell tingled. Did she have another customer? She was going to have to order more pamphlets and maps. It had been manic with the weekend day-trippers wandering in and out. Before she had time to check, the hidden bookshelf door flew open with a bang. Tammy burst through, her face flushed and eyes wild. She waved her phone in the air. "I found her!"

*Could this be the breakthrough we've been hoping for?*

Tammy slammed her phone onto the table, and the screen glowed with promise. She jabbed her finger at the screen. "This is her—Eleanor Cross, freshman at Willowcroft High in 1954."

Olivia leaned in, peering at the young girl's shyness. "So innocent. Only fifteen."

Mrs. Temperance reached in, swiping to the next photos. Her eyes misted over. "Well, I'll be... young love. Takes me back to my dear Harold, God rest his soul. We were high school sweethearts too."

Olivia reminisced about her own first love. Delicious, yes, but a disaster.

"Makes you wonder if she married her Tom after graduation," Tammy said.

*This is where I shine.* "I researched Eleanor Cross while you were gone." Olivia consulted her notepad. "I found a marriage certificate between Eleanor Cross and *Thomas* Bennett in 1957. Right here in Willowcroft."

Tammy gasped. "Our Eleanor and Tom!"

Mrs. Temperance clapped her wrinkled hands. "Well, isn't that darling? Those two lovebirds got hitched." She shook her head. "That's why no one knew an older Eleanor Cross. She's been Mrs. Bennett for decades!"

Olivia peered at her notes. "There's more! I found a Thomas Bennett death fifteen years ago in Lakeview. I only have access to the index which includes name, date of death, and where registered. To access the full certificate, I would have to go into the county offices." She pushed her glasses higher on her nose. "But here's the kicker—I haven't found a death record for Eleanor Bennett. If she was Tom's wife, she may still be alive somewhere in Greater Willowcroft."

Olivia basked in her ability to contribute to the investigation. *Who knew genealogy could be so... detective-y?*

"As it so happens," said Mrs. Temperance, "I met a Mrs. Bennett the other day at Serenity Gardens. It must be her."

Olivia squealed before covering her mouth with her hand to prevent even more high-pitched noises from escaping. Was the only witness still alive?

Olivia hung on every word as Mrs. Temperance recounted her nursing home visit.

"Everything was going well until this young man, Nathan, walked by. He didn't speak, just gave Mrs. Bennett a piercing stare, and she crumbled. Dropped her scone, got all flustered. Wouldn't say another word."

"Strange," Olivia said, her imagination cooking up a dozen scenarios. Did they know each other? Was he threatening her? "Do you think he's tied to Mrs. Bennett's past or whatever secret she's hiding?"

Mrs. Temperance tugged at a ball of wool. "I can't say for certain, but we should keep an eye out for any link between them."

"Agreed," said Wally. "We're not ruling out any possibilities yet."

*Is Mrs. Bennett also Eleanor Cross? What's Nathan's role in all of this? He's too young to have been involved in the original murder. Is he a clue or a red herring?*

"Mark my words," Mrs. Temperance said, "that boy knows something important, something about Mrs. Bennett."

Olivia's curiosity was eating at her. "We must find out what it is. I feel a breakthrough simmering!"

"We need to talk to Eleanor," said Tammy, standing. "Come on, Mrs. Temperance. Let's go now."

Startled, Mrs. Temperance set down her knitting. "O-okay dear, give me a minute."

Lockie stood ready to dash off. Olivia scooped him up and held him tight. "How about you stay with me? I need a cuddle. My curiosity is at a rolling boil, and you know what they say about cats and curiosity. We're safer here together."

Lockie looked at her as if to say, 'sorry I'm not yours,' and ran after Tammy and Mrs. Temperance. *Well, Olivia, that's what you get when you try to commandeer someone else's cat.* A pang of loneliness hit her. *Maybe it's time to find my own furball to keep me company?*

To distract herself, she picked up the photos Xander had printed and added them to their murder board. What had young Eleanor witnessed? Was Max Cross her father? Did he support his daughter? Did Eleanor lean on Tom? They must have married right after high school, if only three years after she was a freshman. *Come on, Olivia, think!*

Softness smacked against Olivia's face. "What the?" She rubbed her cheek and saw a ball of wool bounce away.

Wally chuckled.

"You disappeared into a trance," said Xander. "Anything you'd like to share?"

# Chapter 18

Tammy and Mrs. Temperance rushed across the square and past Mrs. Temperance's house on their way to the nursing home. With the initial adrenaline rush subsiding, Tammy doubted her plan to visit Mrs. Bennett. "Are we sure this is a good idea? What if she doesn't want to talk to us?"

Mrs. Temperance sighed, her wise gaze unwavering. "It's a gamble we must take. Eleanor Cross's knowledge is crucial."

Tammy hesitated for a moment, then nodded. "It can't hurt to see what she has to say."

As they entered the reception area of the nursing home, the smell of antiseptic mingled with a hint of stale air, and the distant sound of a television drifted down the hallway.

"Tread lightly," Mrs. Temperance said. "We mustn't frighten her."

"Understood," Tammy replied, falling into step behind her. Muffled sounds grew louder as they approached the common room.

In the corner sat an elderly woman, lost in thought, her eyes fixed on something outside. Could this delicate figure be the key to Mary's murder?

"Eleanor?" Mrs. Temperance said.

The woman turned, uncertainty clouding her pale blue eyes. Mrs. Temperance gave a warm smile, with a glint in her eye. Ah, clever Mrs. Temperance—using the first name to confirm if this was Eleanor Cross.

"I'm Hazel Temperance. We met the other day, remember? This is my friend Tammy."

Recognition flickered across Eleanor's face. "Of course. Of course. Please, sit."

Tammy studied the woman as they sat. She was tiny, her skin almost translucent under the fluorescent lights. Years of experience etched every wrinkle, and the weight of secrets lurked behind her eyes.

"How are you today, dear? We were hoping to talk for a bit," Mrs. Temperance said gently.

Eleanor tugged at her sleeves with trembling hands as her eyes darted around the room before answering. "I-I'm all right."

Sympathy pulled at Tammy's heart. What had Eleanor endured all these years?

Mrs. Temperance pressed in. "I know it's difficult, but we need to ask you about what happened in 1954. You are Eleanor Cross, aren't you?"

Anguish flashed across Eleanor's face, her features contorted as though battling an internal demon. Fear radiated from her. But of what? Or whom? With a shaky breath and downcast eyes, Eleanor spoke, "It was a long time ago." Her hands twisted the frayed edges of her cardigan. "Yes, I was Eleanor Cross." She lifted her eyes and scanned the room.

Sweat formed on the old woman's brow. Tammy softened her voice. "Can you recall giving a statement to the sheriff back in 1954 about a murder at the little blue cottage?" Tammy stilled her tapping feet and pressed her lips together to stop the barrage of questions she wanted answers to.

Mrs. Bennett fidgeted with her skirt. Tammy followed her flitting gaze. Was she searching for something? Or someone? Despite the apprehension, Tammy saw determination.

"Y-yes, I remember," she said, her eyes returning to Tammy's. "It's not something one easily forgets."

"Would you mind sharing what you saw that night?" Mrs. Temperance said, reaching out to place a comforting hand on Mrs. Bennett's arm.

Taking a deep breath, Mrs. Bennett seemed to gather her courage. "Well, I was walking my dog..." Her face paled, her gaze shifting to something behind them.

Tammy turned to see what had caused such a reaction. A young man in his early twenties stood there, wearing a hoodie zipped and pulled over his head despite the summer weather. Mrs. Temperance whispered that this was Nathan, the boy from her previous visit. He was pushing a wheelchair occupied by an elderly man, likely his grandfather, into the common room.

"Talking isn't always wise," Nathan's words boomed across the room as his eyes bored into Eleanor. "Sometimes, it's better to keep quiet." Was that a threat?

Nathan maneuvered closer. He shot a calculating glance at the trio before his expression transformed into a leer directed at Mrs. Bennett. His grandfather, eyes rheumy and distant, babbled two or three words before relapsing into silence.

"Mum's the word," he said. "No good ever came from digging up old bones."

The boy wheeled the wheelchair forward. Eleanor shrank into her chair, hands squeezed tight, eyes shifting nervously from the boy to the old man.

Tammy studied the old woman's face, reading the naked fear. Who was she afraid of—Nathan or his grandfather? What power did they have over her?

"Actually, I... don't know what you're talking about," Mrs. Bennett said extra loud. Fingers twisted in her lap and her gaze alternated between Nathan and Mrs. Temperance, betraying her inner turmoil.

Tammy exchanged a puzzled glance with Mrs. Temperance. *What is going on? What do we do now?* Other residents' voices grew louder, increasing the tension.

Tammy bit her lip. She yearned to push further, to uncover the truth behind Mrs. Bennett's statement, but doing so might endanger the fragile woman. Mrs. Temperance mirrored her concern.

"Perhaps we should let you be," Tammy suggested, offering Mrs. Bennett an escape without arousing suspicion. Relief flickered across the older woman's face before she masked it with a nod.

"Yes, that would be best," she agreed. "My memory isn't what it used to be." An unconvincing smile appeared on her face. The fear in her eyes belied her words.

Tammy's gaze shifted to Nathan. His eyes were glued on the three women as he listened to each word, every muscle taut. One hand gripped the wheelchair while the other remained hidden.

Mrs. Temperance rose. "I'm sorry we bothered you, Mrs. Bennett. We'll be going now."

Tammy appreciated Mrs. Temperance putting an end to the awkward standoff. She'd been focusing on Nathan and wanted more time with him. But they had to retreat for Eleanor's sake, potentially even her safety. The investigation had taken a sinister turn.

"Come along, Tammy," Mrs. Temperance said. "Take care, Eleanor."

Tammy stood to leave. Her eyes stayed on Nathan. His shoulders lowered as they walked away, but his gaze remained icy. What was he hiding? How could she coax Eleanor's secret from her? Were they close? Why did he have to ruin it?

"That boy is trouble," Mrs. Temperance muttered.

"We need to find the nurse and report this. Maybe she can shed light on Nathan's interest in Mrs. Bennett."

At the nurses' station, a tired-looking woman in black scrubs hunched over a computer.

"Excuse me," Tammy said. "We just had a strange encounter while visiting Eleanor Bennett. Could we discuss it with you?"

The nurse acknowledged them. "Of course. Step into the office."

She led them into a cramped room cluttered with folders and posters about handwashing techniques.

"Is Mrs. Bennett okay?" the woman asked, folding her hands atop a stack of papers.

"Physically, yes," Tammy said, "but there was an incident with another resident's grandson, Nathan. He brought his relative into the common room and seemed to be eavesdropping on our conversation."

"His presence terrified Mrs. Bennett," added Mrs. Temperance. "We're worried about her."

"Nathan's been here daily for weeks now, but he's never upset Mrs. Bennett before," the nurse said, frowning. "He sits with his grandfather for hours, even though the poor man can barely string two words together. He scribbles away in a little notebook, like he's keeping an account of everything he hears. Sometimes, he acts more frustrated than anything, like he's trying to solve a puzzle." She shook her head. "Never thought much of it until now. Dementia patients often revert to the past talking about their childhood or old friends. I can't imagine why that should upset Mrs. Bennett."

"Taking notes?" Mrs. Temperance said.

Tammy turned to Mrs. Temperance, whose eyebrows mirrored her own confusion. Olivia might suggest it was about family history, but was that the whole story?

"Yes," the woman said. "I don't know what his intentions are, but it's unsettling if it's affecting Mrs. Bennett."

The obsessive notetaking seemed suspicious. What was Nathan so intent on documenting? And why was he eager for his grandfather's words, but not Mrs. Bennett's?

Tammy ended the conversation, sensing there was nothing further to glean. "Thank you for speaking with us," Tammy said. "We'll try to return when Nathan's not here."

They thanked the nurse and headed out.

Nathan's presence had stopped Mrs. Bennett from divulging information about a murder. They'd have to outwit the young man to uncover the truth.

"What do you think Nathan's up to?" Mrs. Temperance asked. "Don't tell me nursing homes are like high school with cool kids and bullies. No one should relive their teens."

Tammy shuddered at the thought. She would never want to go through that stage again, no matter how much older and wiser she was. "I agree with you there."

"And why is he so interested in the ramblings?"

"I'm not sure. But we can't ignore how he frightened Mrs. Bennett. There's clearly more at play here."

"We must be careful. I think we're stumbling upon information someone wants buried."

Tammy tried to make the pieces fit. "Could Nathan's grandfather be the figure Eleanor saw in her witness statement?"

"Perhaps, but even in a wheelchair, you can see he's tall. And Eleanor Cross described a short person running away."

"True," Tammy agreed, the thought nagging at her. "We'll have to try again when Nathan isn't here." She glanced around, wishing Lockie was with them. *Where is he?*

"I wonder what Lockie would have thought of him? He has this incredible ability to sense things. I've seen him bring out the best in people, but hiss and bristle at those with darker souls."

Mrs. Temperance's eyes twinkled. "Animals often have a sixth sense about these things. My late husband's dog could always predict a storm, long before the first clouds appeared."

Tammy pictured Lockie's eyes narrowing as he assessed Nathan. "I bet Lockie would have arched his back and puffed out his tail the moment he saw Nathan. He might have even positioned himself protectively in front of Mrs. Bennett."

"Or perhaps," Mrs. Temperance added, "he would have stalked Nathan, watching his every move. Cats can be quite the little detectives."

Nathan skulked out of the nursing home. His heart thudded like a war drum as he followed the women. *Not too close. Don't let them see you.* He strained to overhear the conversation. Do they know about his grandfather's cryptic ramblings? How did they find Eleanor?

He wanted to sit with his notebook and string the sentences together to solve the puzzle. The details had to stay within the family—those meddling old biddies would not ruin this.

As they reached the town square, Nathan ducked behind a tree. The women crossed the square and entered the bookstore. Dang it! He couldn't follow them inside. Perspiration beads formed on his forehead.

He hurried to the fountain, hoping to observe without being detected. What were they plotting with Eleanor? What did she tell them? How much had his grandpa let slip? *No, focus. There's still time. I'm close. So close.*

Nathan clenched his fists. He would have to step up his game—threats, lies, or worse—he'd silence them all. The truth was his to uncover, his alone.

Tammy and Mrs. Temperance went through to the back room. The others remained gathered around the table in their makeshift headquarters.

"Any news?" Olivia asked.

"Plenty," Tammy replied. "But we're not sure what it means."

Tammy summarized their nursing home visit. "Nathan's behavior is certainly suspicious. He seemed very invested in keeping his grandfather's ramblings secret... oops!" Tammy stamped her foot and her hands formed fists. "We don't know his name. I could kick myself." Tammy swung a leg through the air. *You numbskull. There's your proof, Mother.* She turned to Mrs. Temperance. "We didn't ask for his name. He's more than 'Nathan's grandfather.'"

Wally crossed his arms. "Never mind that for now. Is Nathan involved somehow? Protecting his grandfather all these years later?"

"It's possible," Tammy said, still disappointed with herself and her mother's words bouncing around in her head. "But he's a tall man, so he can't be the man Eleanor saw running away."

"Perhaps there's something or someone else we've yet to discover," said Mrs. Temperance.

Wally stroked his chin, considering the information. "What if Mrs. Bennett lied to move suspicion away from the real murderer, or—"

An ear-splitting crash of shattering glass erupted.

# Chapter 19

The crash flooded Olivia with memories of the bear visit. Had her window been shattered again? At least she wasn't alone this time. Chairs toppled as everyone sprang to their feet in alarm.

"Stay here," Wally commanded, as he hurried toward the store to investigate.

*Stay here? Fat chance.* Curiosity overpowered her sense of caution, as usual. She'd already faced a bear. Besides, it was her store. Her responsibility.

The familiar throb of an oncoming headache pulsed behind her eyes as she followed Wally. The others were close behind. Shards of glass littered the floor like glittering daggers. Olivia spied the gaping hole—a punch to the gut. She cataloged the damage and calculated the costs.

"Not again!" said Olivia. "It's less than a week old!" She bent down and played with a shard or two, her teary eyes surveying the mess. *I'm going to have to close...again.*

A brick lay among the debris, an unwelcome intruder. First a bear, now this? Two weeks ago, her biggest worry had been which novels to feature in the window display. Now, she was caught in some bizarre mash-up of a cozy mystery and a thriller. Was this the price of adventure?

Mrs. Temperance's gasp brought Olivia back into the moment. "Who would do such a thing?"

Wally's jaw tightened. "Someone who doesn't want us snooping."

Olivia's stomach scrambled as she turned the brick over. An elastic band held a scrap of paper in place, like a sinister gift tag. She extracted the note. Jagged letters screamed their message: STOP ASKING QUESTIONS OR ELSE!

The threat was clear. This was no longer a fun mystery to solve over hot cocoa. Whoever threw it knew they were investigating and wanted to keep the truth buried. Olivia's hand quivered as she held the warning. *Is this really happening?* Fear crept in. *Have we gone too far?*

Lockie, always in tune with people's emotions, brushed against her leg, offering support. "No honey this time, Lockie," she said and gave him a pat.

"Nathan?" Tammy asked.

"We've rattled someone's cage," Wally said.

"He must have followed us here," said Mrs. Temperance.

"Seems likely," said Wally.

Regaining her composure, Olivia contributed to the conversation. "Maybe Nathan's grandfather let something slip," she ventured, sounding stronger than she felt. "Something Nathan wants to keep buried. And Mrs. Bennett overheard?"

Tammy bit her lip. "Possibly. We know he was talking about the past. Perhaps he said something incriminating."

"And Nathan picked up on it," Wally finished. "He's been taking notes on his grandfather's ramblings to discover the truth."

"If his grandfather confessed a role in Mary's murder, even unintentionally, Nathan would definitely want us out of the way," Tammy said, her eyes wide. "He's protecting his grandfather."

Olivia glanced around the room, noting the uneasy expressions on everyone's faces. "I think Nathan knows something we don't."

"Yep," Xander said, "we're missing key pieces of this puzzle."

"Exactly," Tammy nodded. "And Mrs. Bennett knows something Nathan doesn't want her to tell us."

"We need to find out what that is," Xander said, "before he finds a way to silence Mrs. Bennett for good."

"Which means Mrs. Bennett is in danger," Olivia said, a hand flying to cover her mouth. Had they stirred up enough trouble to get someone killed? It was meant to be a cold case.

"We have to get to Mrs. Bennett before Nathan does," Tammy declared. "She's the key to unlocking this mystery."

Mrs. Temperance tapped on her phone. "I'm calling the nursing home," she said, her usual composure cracking. Xander showed Mrs. Temperance how to put it on speakerphone as they huddled around, the shards of glass crunching beneath their feet.

"Serenity Gardens. How may I help you?"

"Hello, Emma? This is Mrs. Temperance. I was wondering if you could tell me if young Nathan is still there?"

There was a moment of dead air. "He left not long after you did. In quite the hurry."

"Really?" Mrs. Temperance said. "Is Mrs. Bennett all right?"

"Nathan spoke with Mrs. Bennett before he left."

Mrs. Temperance pursed her lips. "Did he now? Can you please check on Mrs. Bennett? Nathan upsets her and I want to make sure she's okay."

"Of course. Let me find her." The line went quiet.

The knot in Olivia's stomach tightened as the silence stretched. Her teeth found her thumbnail, gnawing until she tasted copper. What was taking so long?

Finally, the line crackled back to life. "Oh my, it seems Nathan did a number on the poor woman. She was in hysterics. We had to sedate her. I find it strange Nathan would have such an effect on Mrs. Bennett. They used to get along so well."

The statement puzzled Olivia. She exchanged glances with the others.

"But why would Nathan talk to Mrs. Bennett at all?" Mrs. Temperance asked.

"Mrs. Bennett and Nathan's grandfather, Max, are siblings. That makes Nathan a sort of nephew... her great-nephew, I guess."

Olivia's mouth fell agape. As she surveyed the scene, she saw the same shock mirrored on everyone's faces. Nathan's grandfather was Max Cross.

"Hello?... Hello? Is anyone there?" came over the phone's speaker.

Mrs. Temperance tried to speak. "Yes... sorry... P-please take good care of Mrs. Bennett. We'll come visit later once the sedative has worn off. Thank you."

Xander ended the call.

The conversation left Olivia reeling. Mrs. Bennett and Nathan's grandfather were Eleanor and Max Cross, brother and sister. Olivia's genealogy should have figured that out, but she'd focused her searches on Eleanor rather than Max. *A rookie mistake I won't repeat.*

"What if it was Max Mrs. Bennett saw?" she speculated. "Max might have threatened her into keeping quiet, then made her lie about what she saw to turn suspicion away from himself."

Mrs. Temperance had a slight tear in her eye. "Eleanor had to live with that her whole life. And now they're in the same nursing home. She must have felt safe with his dementia. But now, he's babbling, and Nathan's figured it out."

This wasn't just about solving a mystery. It was about protecting a woman who had carried a terrible burden for most of her life.

"Nathan must have threatened Mrs. Bennett after we left," Tammy speculated, clenching her fists. "We need to find a way to talk to her without him finding out."

"Agreed," Xander said. "But how do we do that? And how can we ensure Mrs. Bennett's safety?"

"There's more at stake here than we thought," said Mrs. Temperance.

"Let's think this through," Wally suggested, scratching his chin. "We have to assume Nathan will be keeping tabs on us, so any visit we make to the nursing home would be discovered." Wally took charge in his Sheriff Wallace voice, "Xander, you stay here with Olivia. Help her clean up and keep an eye on things while we're gone."

Xander bobbed his head as he straightened his posture. "Got it."

"Tammy, Mrs. Temperance, come with me. I'll drive you over to Serenity Gardens to make sure you're there when Mrs. Bennett's sedative wears off. We need to get to the bottom of this." Wally's authoritative manner left no room for argument. "Then I'll head to the sheriff's station and update them on everything we have."

Wally, Mrs. Temperance, and Tammy headed out the back door to Wally's car. Lockie lagged behind. Olivia wanted to go with them, but the store had to be her priority. That didn't stop her from speculating.

"What I don't understand is why Nathan is taking notes?" Olivia faced Xander. "Surely he'd want no evidence of what his grandfather did."

*Think, Olivia. There has to be a logical explanation here.*

Xander shrugged. "Maybe it's the only way he can make sense of his grandfather's ramblings."

"Hmm." She glared at the shard-covered floor. "It's like déjà vu, isn't it? I'll go get dustpans and brooms."

The trio piled into Wally's SUV and sped toward the nursing home. Tammy fidgeted with her hands as she tried to make sense of all the information they had gathered so far.

What was Nathan writing in his mysterious notebook? And most importantly—what secret was Eleanor so terrified to reveal?

The sun inched closer to the horizon—time was running out.

As they entered the building, Nurse Emma greeted them, concern etched on her face. Tammy suspected they exuded frantic energy.

"How is Mrs. Bennett?" Mrs. Temperance asked without stopping for pleasantries. "Has she woken yet?"

The nurse sighed. "Not yet. That nephew of hers did a number on her."

Tammy clenched her fists at the thought of poor Mrs. Bennett being stuck in the same nursing home as the brother who bullied her seventy years earlier. "We're going to wait in her room until she wakes."

The two women marched down the hall, the distant piano music clashing with the rhythm of their steps. Tammy's focus remained on the woman who held the key to unlocking the mysteries of her cottage.

Arriving at Mrs. Bennett's room, Mrs. Temperance said, "Let's get the truth."

They were on the precipice of something monumental. Tammy knocked on the door before opening it.

Heavy curtains blocked out the daylight. In the dimness, she made out a figure looming over Eleanor Bennett's motionless form.

Tammy's breath caught in her throat. A cold sweat broke out on her forehead as her palms turned clammy.

The figure whipped around.

A face contorted with rage—Nathan.

His outstretched arms held a pillow over Eleanor's face in a murderous grip.

# Chapter 20

Mrs. Bennett's frail body lay still, not resisting Nathan's smothering. Hazel's veins ran cold. "Stop!" she yelled. "Get away from her!"

Nathan snarled, dropped the pillow, and shoved past Hazel and Tammy, knocking them to the floor. The impact jarred Hazel, but concern for Eleanor propelled her to her feet.

"Help!" Tammy screamed, scrambling on wobbly legs. "I'll go after Nathan. You take care of Mrs. Bennett."

Hazel tried to process the chaos as Tammy sprinted after Nathan. She spotted Nurse Emma in the corridor.

"Emma!" Mrs. Temperance wailed.

The nurse turned in time to dodge Nathan barreling past, with Tammy close behind. The nurse's eyes widened as she headed in Mrs. Bennett's direction.

Hazel rushed to Eleanor's side, grasping her hand. "Please, be okay," she prayed, feeling helpless.

Emma hurried in. She pressed the emergency buzzer on the wall, starting an alarm. Within seconds, the room filled with nurses and orderlies, the air buzzing with their rapid movements.

"Call an ambulance," Emma instructed the first nurse. "Oxygen," she ordered the second.

The new nurse opened a panel on the wall, revealing an outlet. They secured a mask over Mrs. Bennett's pale face, her breaths shallow, the sedation still in effect.

Hazel stood to the side, her body shivering. The flurry of activity around Eleanor brought a mixture of relief and anxiety. She found the strength to explain what had happened. "Nathan was holding a pillow over Eleanor's face. You need to call the sheriff."

Tammy raced after Nathan, her hair whipping behind her. "Stop, Nathan!" she shouted, her breath coming in ragged gasps as she navigated the hallways. "You won't get away with this!"

She spurred her legs to move faster, despite the burning in her muscles.

Nathan's path of destruction lay before her—upended carts, scattered equipment, and frightened faces. She vaulted over obstacles, refusing to let him escape.

Residents cowered in doorways. A nurse pressed herself against the wall, clutching a clipboard to her chest like a shield. Tammy's lungs screamed for air as she struggled to keep pace with Nathan's longer strides.

A terrified wheelchair-bound resident became caught in the crossfire. In panic, they struggled to maneuver out of each other's way. Time slowed as Tammy tried to navigate around him, her fatigue-addled brain unable to coordinate her movements. They engaged in an awkward dance, each move blocked by the other's attempts to clear the path.

"I'm sorry," Tammy said, holding the wheelchair still so she could get around it. But the delay had cost her. Nathan had disappeared.

Her legs grew heavy, each step a monumental effort. The distant wail of sirens offered a glimmer of hope—help was coming. But would it be in time? "Come on, Tammy," she urged herself, pushing through the fatigue threatening to overwhelm her. *You can't let him get away.*

She rounded a corner to find a deserted corridor lined with closed doors.

"Where did you go?" she said, panting, her frustration growing.

A few feet away, a door creaked ajar. Had she found him? Without thinking, Tammy burst inside.

Strong hands slammed against her back, propelling her forward. The force sent her careening toward an unyielding surface, her forehead taking a direct hit. An explosion of pain reverberated through her skull.

Stars exploded behind her eyes as falling objects clattered to the floor. Tammy's vision swam, and she fought to maintain her balance.

The door slammed shut with an ominous click, plunging her into darkness.

Cursing herself for falling into Nathan's trap and for getting injured in the process, she stumbled around for a light switch. A supply closet came into focus. Her fists pounded on the door, but it wouldn't budge. "Let me out!" The chaos in the corridors drowned out her pleas. She was trapped while Nathan escaped.

Sirens grew louder in the distance. Ambulance? Police? Hopefully both. Not that she was any help anymore. Images of Mrs. Bennett's helpless body filled her head.

"You've failed," her mother taunted her. *Nathan's gotten away, and who knows what he'll do next?* Tammy squeezed her eyes shut, trying to block out the intrusive thoughts. But with the sharp tang of blood on her tongue and a throbbing ache spreading from the lump forming on her forehead, hope felt out of reach.

Defeated, she slid to the cold, unforgiving floor while the faint hum of fluorescent lights buzzed overhead. She pulled her knees to her chest in a futile attempt at comfort.

Paramedics pushed past Hazel into the room, their movements swift and precise as they surrounded Mrs. Bennett. One pressed a stethoscope against Eleanor's chest, while another secured tubes and machines to her slight body. The steady beep of the heart monitor came to life.

Memories of Harold springing into action during past emergencies flooded Hazel's mind, his calm efficiency a stark contrast to the current frenzy. The rapid pace of their actions heightened the fear Hazel held for her friend's wellbeing.

"Thank you for coming." Hazel wrung her hands as she watched them work. Was Eleanor going to be okay?

"We're doing everything we can, ma'am," one replied. "She's stable for now, but we're taking her to the hospital for further observation."

Hazel's stomach lurched as they wheeled the gurney out of the room. She followed with quick steps matching her racing heart. Was Tammy safe? Did she catch up with Nathan? Where was the sheriff?

Hazel swept the hallway, searching for her friend. And what about Lockie? Had he not joined them? Was he following Nathan? A cold dread gnawed at her. *Something's not right. Where is Tammy?*

Guilt washed over her. *I should have never encouraged the investigation. This is all my fault.*

Nathan sprinted away from the supply closet, his breaths coming in sharp, panicked gasps. Things hadn't gone to plan. No one was supposed to discover what he was doing. Anxiety clawed at his insides as he slipped into an empty stairwell, pulling the door shut with jittering hands.

Leaning against the cold concrete wall, he tried to steady his breathing, but fear held tight. Images of his grandfather—eyes distant, muttering fragments of the past—flashed before him. Nathan was finally deciphering the old man's ramblings, uncovering a dangerous thread of a past best left forgotten.

*If they find out what he did... what he covered up...* A fresh wave of panic hit. His fingers twitched as he considered the implications. His family's legacy hung in the balance.

*I can't let them get in the way.* The thought came unbidden, tinged with desperation. It wasn't just about his grandfather; it was about preventing anyone else from getting their hands on what belonged to their family.

His notebook held everything—a compilation of his grandfather's disjointed confessions, recorded three or four words at a time. The pieces still hadn't quite fit into place. There were details missing. But the clues pointed to one location.

He doubted they'd figured it out, but they were close on his heels. If they had the answers he didn't, his discovery would be too late. He had to find the hiding place first.

The voices in the hallway grew louder. Nathan stiffened. Were they approaching the stairwell? *Time's running out.* Adrenaline hardened his resolve. If they wouldn't stop digging, he'd have to make them stop.

He hated resorting to violence, but they left him no choice. If only they'd stayed out of his way, none of this would be necessary.

With one last deep breath, Nathan pushed off the wall and slipped out the stairwell's emergency exit, disappearing into the ripening apple orchards beyond. The distant wail of sirens spurred him to sprint—back to the cottage on the edge of town.

"I'm not listening, Mother." The thought came sharp and unbidden. Her mom was in a California nursing home miles away—that didn't stop her words from invading Tammy's thoughts.

"Focus, Tammy." *You need to get out of here.*

She braced herself against the floor and pushed up, fighting for balance. Towering shelves of medical supplies hemmed her in. A clock ticked inside her head, reminding her of the urgency of the situation. One exit.

Pain radiated from the growing lump. The metallic taste of blood from biting her lip lingered. The sound of a faint meow focused her attention on the sound's direction. Had Lockie followed them?

A second meow.

"Lockie, is that you?"

Following the meows, she spotted a small, high window behind boxes of gloves. She might be small enough to squeeze through if she could get to it.

A deafening alarm reverberated through the room. Tammy covered her ears. Had Nathan set off the fire alarm? She braced for the overhead sprinklers, but no water came. That was the last thing she needed. Nathan must have activated an alarmed exit door, meaning he had left the building.

Tammy resumed her focus on the window. With no other option available, she had to make it work.

She positioned a step stool under the window. She climbed up, but even on her tiptoes, it was out of reach. She moved the boxes blocking it then checked the shelves for anything to stand on to give her extra inches.

She spied a sturdy bucket. Tammy dragged it over and placed it upside down on the stool. She held her breath and stepped onto the makeshift platform. Her pulsating head made her clumsy.

The bucket wobbled one way under her weight, and she wobbled the other way, but it held. Her hands shook from exertion and fear. Now able to reach the window, Tammy opened it. Fresh air rushed in, along with a wave of relief. She used the shelves to hoist herself toward the window and squeezed and wiggled herself halfway through.

A flashlight blinded her. What the?

"Hey. Stop right there!"

# Chapter 21

Tammy froze. Was it the sheriff? Her current predicament made her look guilty. "I know what you're thinking, but Nathan locked me in here. It's him you need to find." She tried to wiggle through further.

"Stop moving!"

She could just make out his hand hovering over a holstered weapon. "Sorry. Sorry. I'm not a threat." Her voice was strained from her awkward position. "I'm Tammy Rumbelow and my friend Wally was the one who called you to help."

He hesitated for a moment before lowering his hand and motioning to his partner to assist. They helped Tammy climb down from the window, her legs trembling.

"Thank you." Lockie jumped into Tammy's arms, pressing his forehead against her cheek in a gentle headbutt. "It *was* you I heard. Thanks for the assist."

She turned to the deputies. "We have to find Nathan—he's dangerous. He tried to kill Mrs. Bennett."

She explained how Nathan had locked her in the supply closet after attacking Mrs. Bennett.

"I need to find my friend Mrs. Temperance. She stayed with Mrs. Bennett when I chased after Nathan. Are they okay?"

The officer laid a reassuring hand on Tammy's shoulder. "Mrs. Bennett has been taken to the hospital, but she's going to be okay thanks to your friend's quick actions. Mrs. Temperance is over there speaking with some of my colleagues."

He pointed across the parking lot to where Mrs. Temperance stood talking to two deputies. A wave of relief crashed over her.

"Now we need to get your head checked. That golf ball is becoming a tennis ball." He walked her over to an ambulance, then excused himself.

With her eyesight returning after the blinding glare of the deputies and the paramedic's torch, Tammy took in the chaotic scene. She'd thought inside was mayhem. The scene outside resembled an octogenarian rodeo as nurses and deputies tried to corral a bunch of spry seniors who, embracing their unexpected freedom, used walkers and canes to aid fellow residents' escapes. The red and blue lights of ambulances and squad cars swirling in the dark gave it a disco-like atmosphere.

She laughed. At least some people found a silver lining in the night's drama.

"Ms. Rumbelow, I'm Deputy Brown." The introduction brought back the real reason for their presence. "When you're ready, we need your statement." His tone was both stern and compassionate.

She nodded, her gaze alternating between the deputy and Mrs. Temperance across the way.

"Of course, Officer. I want to help."

As they walked over to Mrs. Temperance, Tammy overheard her telling them about Mary.

"We believe this attack on Mrs. Bennett is related to an unsolved murder from 1954. Mrs. Bennett was a witness, and we think Max Cross, Nathan's grandfather, was somehow involved, maybe even the killer."

"Is there any evidence to support this theory?"

Tammy answered as they approached, "Not yet, but we're close."

"Sheriff Stanton, this is Tammy who bought the little blue cottage," Mrs. Temperance said.

"Ah, so you're our new resident."

"It seems everyone was expecting me." She stifled an eye roll as she spoke. No chance of a stealthy arrival in this town. "We've been investigating Mary's murder, and every clue seems to lead back to the same place: the Cross family. Max Cross is Mrs. Bennett's brother."

The officer appeared skeptical, but took note of their statements. "We'll look into it. In the meantime, report anything else you find to us immediately. And if what you've said is true, with Nathan on the loose, you ladies may still be in danger," Stanton said. "We'll provide security details until he's apprehended."

Tammy's stomach plummeted. This is all her fault. If she hadn't snooped... If she hadn't involved Mrs. Temperance... Mrs. Bennett wouldn't need a hospital. No security required.

With the adrenaline fading, her misshapen head pounded. What a mess. True mysteries are dangerous. *I should stick to writing fake ones. I nearly got someone killed. More evidence for my mother to taunt me with.*

"Are there any leads on where Nathan is?" Tammy asked.

"We have deputies combing the area," Stanton explained. "But so far, no sign of him."

Protection sounded good.

The officers dispersed to continue their investigation. Their radios crackled as they fanned out into the night. Would they catch Nathan before he struck again?

Mrs. Temperance turned to her. "I'm so glad you are safe. I was worried about what would happen if you caught Nathan." She gestured toward the swelling. "I see by your forehead you put yourself in harm's way to protect Mrs. Bennett."

A surge of emotion rose in her throat, swelling in tandem with the lump on her head. She wanted to shield herself from toxic relationships behind a protective wall. Yet, as she gazed at Mrs. Temperance, she understood Willowcroft had gifted her more than a mystery to unravel. It had given her genuine friendships, trust, and bonds forged in shared adventure and danger.

"I'm just glad you're both safe," Tammy said, her voice cracking. "I don't know what I would have done if something had happened to you or Mrs. Bennett. Your friendship has meant more to me than you know."

Mrs. Temperance took Tammy's hand. "I'm proud to call you my friend."

Butterflies exploded inside Tammy. She had been pushing people away, afraid of being hurt or betrayed, but Mrs. Temperance's unwavering support and genuine care had shown her true friendships did exist.

Standing there surrounded by sirens and elderly escapees, she realized returning to her LA life was no longer an option.

"There you are!" Wally said, striding toward them. His confident presence lifted the burden off Tammy.

He took in the surrounding chaos. "I dropped Olivia at the station. The broken window has dredged up memories from the bear visit. She's giving a statement—"

A determined ninety-year-old shuffled past, waving his cane in the air like a victory flag, shouting "Freedom!"

"What is going on here?" asked Wally. By now, Tammy had accepted the nursing home residents' shenanigans occurring around them as normal.

"I knew something had happened," Wally continued, "when I saw everyone in the sheriff's building spring into action, leaving only Deputy Scott behind."

A wry smile tugged at one corner of his mouth. "I'm not sure who was more stunned—Olivia or Deputy Scott." A sly chuckle escaped. "I figured Olivia's instincts would kick in if anything happened and she'd protect Scott."

Mrs. Temperance snorted a laugh.

"I've sent young Xander home." Wally turned to Tammy. "His father's a park ranger, used to wrangling bears, especially after last week's great bear caper. Figured he'd be safe there while we sort out this mess."

"Good thinking." Mrs. Temperance shook her head. "What have I gotten that poor boy into?"

"I aim to keep you all safe," he said. "Everyone's staying at my place tonight—three doors from the sheriff's station."

A slight ease settled into Tammy's muscles, though tension still coiled tight in her neck. The idea of safety felt distant but attainable with Wally's reassurance. "Can I grab a bag of essentials?" Tammy asked. "And I need to find Lockie. He helped me out of the room Nathan locked me in but then took off."

"Of course," said Wally. "I'm sure Lockie is waiting for you at home hiding away from all this noise." He glanced at Tammy's forehead. "We need to get an ice pack for that."

Tammy raised a hand to the bulge, its steady ache impossible to ignore.

"Sheriff Stanton has offered us protection," Mrs. Temperance said.

"Great." He gestured to a paramedic. "You two stay here while I check in with Stanton."

Mrs. Temperance angled closer to Tammy. "With the bear visits and now all this, I bet Sheriff Stanton wishes Wally hadn't retired." She swept her eyes over the scene where the octogenarians appeared to be winning.

Wally returned. "Stanton's sending Brown to collect Olivia and take her to my place. Mrs. Temperance, we'll go to yours first to grab some things."

"Thank you, Wally," she said.

He placed a reassuring hand on Tammy's shoulder. "We'll keep you safe," he promised, his eyes steady and sincere.

Wally led them through the chaotic maze of flashing lights and bustling officers. Tammy pressed the cold pack against the hammering growth, wincing at the sharp sting. The absurdity of the escaping seniors faded behind them. Were they being watched? Followed? Nathan could be anywhere.

Tammy sat in the idling car, biting her lip as she waited while Wally accompanied Mrs. Temperance inside to pack a bag. *This is all my fault. If I hadn't pursued this mystery...* Nathan had already attacked the bookstore. The possibility their homes might be next sent her heart racing.

She fidgeted in her seat, her eyes darting around the darkened street until Mrs. Temperance and Wally returned unharmed. They set off for Tammy's little blue cottage.

From the street, the cottage sat still, its windows dark.

"Lock the doors and stay low," Wally said to Mrs. Temperance as he scanned the perimeter before exiting the car. He glanced at Tammy. "Keep an eye out for anything that moves."

Tammy gnawed the inside of her cheek, her eyes searching for disturbances. The idea of Nathan breaking into her home made her skin crawl. She shoved down the rising fear. She was determined to retrieve Lockie and her belongings.

They took slow, deliberate steps as they crouched along the path. Every crackle of leaves made her jump. She called for Lockie but heard no reply. Her voice quavered, displaying the anxiety she tried to keep in check.

Lockie had become an integral part of her life and Tammy didn't want to imagine life without him now. She might still be stuck in the supply closet if not for him. *Where are you, buddy?* Had something happened to him?

She lifted her eyes to the cottage. Her stomach twisted at the sight of a broken window. The stakes were raised. Did Nathan know where she lived? Was her cottage the site where his grandfather became a murderer? Her private space had never been violated in LA. She'd be safe if she'd stayed there.

"Keep behind me," Wally warned as they reached the porch, his hand hovering over his holster. "We don't know what we'll find inside."

*Am I in danger? Has Lockie been hurt?* How dare Nathan cause all this trouble? *Poor Mary deserves justice, and how else will she get it if we don't solve her murder?*

"Lockie! Here, boy," Tammy called again, to no response. She followed Wally to the front door, her heart pounding.

"Stay close, and be ready for anything," Wally said, as they passed the shattered window.

As they slunk into the cottage, Tammy's senses heightened with every floor-board creak and wind chime tinkle. She hesitated at the entrance to the living room, a place she hadn't dared to enter since seeing the crime scene photos at the bookstore that visualized its gruesome past. When she returned home two nights ago, she had gone straight to the bedroom, deliberately avoiding that room then, and until now.

She entered quaking, the images flashing through her mind. Then she saw it—another brick on the floor with a note.

Wally extricated the letter and read it aloud. "'The money is mine. Back off.'" He handed it to Tammy. "Money? What money?"

Tammy recognized the familiar scrawled and jagged writing from the bookstore note. "Could Max know where the bank heist money is?"

"Whether he does or not, it looks like Nathan believes his grandfather knows, meaning Max was potentially involved. If Mary discovered Max's involvement, that would be a motive for murder."

Before they pondered further, Lockie leaped from the hallway into Tammy's arms, startling her.

"Lockie!" Relief flooded through her as she squeezed her loyal companion. "I was worried about you."

But he wasn't stopping for a reunion cuddle. With an agile twist, he squirmed out of her grasp, bolting to the fireplace. She blinked at his sudden movement. The cat clawed and poked at the stones, his persistence demanding attention.

Could his feline instincts uncover the cottage's secrets? Tammy's gut churned as he scratched.

"That's the second time you've fixated there." *He must be trying to tell me something.*

As she knelt to examine the area, a noise from outside spooked her. Fear resurfaced in Tammy's chest. Was Nathan lurking nearby?

"Grab your overnight bag. We need to get back to Mrs. Temperance," Wally said, his eyes assessing their surroundings, his hand resting on his holster.

Tammy darted into her bedroom, yanking drawers, and stuffing clothes into a bag with shaking hands. Each creak of the house sent a prickling tension up her neck. "Lockie, come on," she urged, but the cat was fixated on the fireplace, his claws scraping against the stone.

"Lockie, please," she begged, scooping him up. He squirmed in her arms, meowing in protest. "We have to go."

From the window, Wally signaled frantically. "We need to leave now!"

She gulped, casting one last glance at the fireplace. Whatever secrets it held would have to wait.

"Okay, I'm ready." Tammy slung her bag over her shoulder and extricated the cat.

"Let's go. We'll be safer at my place."

They dashed to Wally's car. Tammy rapped on the window. Inside, Mrs. Temperance sat bolt upright, eyes wide with alarm.

"It's us."

Mrs. Temperance realized it was them and unlocked the doors. "You scared me out of my wits. What took you so long?"

Lockie jumped into Tammy's lap, nudging his cheek against hers to help calm her nerves. "We got another note."

Behind the wheel, Wally accelerated, gravel skidding beneath the tires as they sped into town. The cottage faded into the distance, swallowed by the night as Tammy updated Mrs. Temperance.

"Oh my, this is getting more dangerous by the minute." Her rosy cheeks had paled. The gravity of the night's events deepened the lines on her face.

"Lockie may have found something," Tammy said.

"Like what?"

"We don't know. We'll have to come back and investigate further once it's safe," she replied, her eyes meeting Lockie's. "We have to figure out how all the pieces fit—the bank robbery, the murder, the letter, Max, Mrs. Bennett, Nathan, and the two notes."

# Chapter 22

Wally's SUV rumbled to a stop in his driveway. Red and blue lights from Deputy Brown's squad car flashed in the night.

A pulsing ache emanated from Tammy's forehead as she threw open the passenger door.

"Thank goodness you're all safe!" Olivia exclaimed, pulling Tammy close.

Tammy melted into Olivia's arms, her shoulders dropping as a long, shuddering breath escaped her lips. The warmth of her friend's embrace seeped through her clothes, thawing the icy grip of fear that had held her. Her clenched jaw relaxed. As Olivia's hand traced soothing circles on her back, Tammy's heartbeat slowed. So much had happened since that first Willowcroft hug from Mrs. Applewood.

"Good to see you all in one piece," Deputy Brown broke the moment of comfort. Tammy reluctantly pulled away from Olivia to acknowledge him.

Lockie sprang from the car and bounded over to Olivia. He reared up on his hind legs, front paws reaching for her attention.

"Well, look at that," Wally chuckled. "Seems Lockie's apologizing for abandoning you earlier."

Olivia scooped up the cat, cuddling him close. "I missed you too, you little rascal." She glanced at Tammy, pointing to the protuberance on her head. "What did I miss?"

Tammy gingerly touched the tender lump. The day's chaotic events flashed through her mind like a horror movie highlight reel: Nathan's crazed eyes as he tried to smother Mrs. Bennett, the click of the supply closet lock trapping her in darkness, the shattering of Olivia's bookstore window, shards of week-old glass littering the floor.

"It's been a hell of a night. We'll fill you in on everything, but I need a cup of tea and about ten ibuprofen."

Wally placed a comforting hand on Tammy's shoulder. "I've updated Brown on the little blue cottage's broken window. He'll radio it in so Stanton can investigate. The cottage will now be a crime scene, like the store and the nursing home."

Mrs. Temperance sighed. "The whole town's going to be covered in yellow tape if we don't catch Nathan soon."

"We predicted Tammy would bring adventure to the town," said Olivia. "This wasn't what I meant, but you have to tell me everything."

"Let's go inside," said Wally. "I'll put the kettle on. Then we can hear all about it."

As the motley crew made their way up the porch steps, Lockie leaped from Olivia's arms and darted ahead. They were safe, for now.

Wally's house sat off the square, like a supporting character. Vintage furnishings mixed with sleek gadgets—a 1950s reading lamp that wouldn't be out of place in Mary's cottage and a state-of-the-art coffee machine. What would her book's sleuth deduce about Wally from this? Outside, Deputy Brown's presence was a sobering reminder this was no fictional tale.

Tammy wrapped her hands around a steaming mug of chamomile tea as she and Mrs. Temperance took turns recounting the night's harrowing events. *Olivia's eyes widened so much I thought they were going to pop out of her head.*

"What is Nathan doing?" Olivia asked, her fingers drumming her mug.

Mrs. Temperance shook her head, her bright shawl slipping. "He thinks he's protecting his grandfather, is my guess."

Tammy rubbed her temples, the throbbing in her head a constant reminder of her own close call. "If we hadn't arrived when we did, I don't even want to think about what might have happened."

"And he locked you in a supply closet?" Olivia asked, her brows knitted.

"I'm just glad I managed to break out, thanks to Lockie," Tammy said, suppressing a shiver at the memory of squeezing through the small window. "But that's not all. When we got back to the cottage, there was another broken window and a note."

She pulled the crumpled paper from her pocket and smoothed it out on the table. The words scowled back at them: The money is mine. Back off.

Olivia inspected the note before leaning back in the chair. "And what about Lockie? You mentioned he was acting strangely near the fireplace?"

Tammy nodded, glancing at the cat snuggled in a chair. "He was pawing at the stones like crazy. He was trying to tell us something. But we got spooked by a noise and left before checking it out."

Tammy tried to join the dots. Nathan's desperate attempt on Mrs. Bennett's life, the cryptic notes, Lockie's odd behavior... it all led to something. But what?

She sipped her tea; the balm soothed her frayed nerves. She needed sleep. Her body ached, and her head pulsed. "We'll start again tomorrow?" she said, scanning the tired faces.

Wally stood, his joints cracking. "I've got two bunk beds in the grandkids' room. They're not fancy, but they're comfortable enough."

*I bet he's a great grandfather. And now he's protecting us like family.* "Thanks, Wally."

Olivia yawned, stretching her arms above her head. "I call top bunk," she said, with a hint of playfulness.

Tammy chuckled, feeling a wave of affection for her resilient friend.

"Bottom bunks are reserved for myself and Mrs. Temperance," Wally said.

"You're not sleeping in your own room?" asked Mrs. Temperance.

"We're safer altogether for now."

"Top it is," said Tammy, hoping her misshapen forehead wouldn't affect her balance on the ladder.

Wally led them to the bedroom, Lockie trailing behind. The bunks had mini staircases rather than ladders, thank goodness.

Tammy climbed to the top bunk, the soft mattress enveloping her aching body. Lockie jumped up beside her, curling into a ball of fur. She stroked his ears, finding comfort in the simple action. "What are you trying to tell us, buddy?"

She glanced at Olivia, asleep on the opposite bunk, worry etched on her face despite her earlier upbeat attitude. Tammy's heart ached for her friend with the bear visit still fresh. Another shattered window, and menacing words.

The covers tangled around Tammy's legs as she tossed and turned. Too hot. Too cold. Nathan's attempt to smother Mrs. Bennett, bricks through windows, sinister notes—it all flashed before her. Lockie shared her restlessness, his black-and-white fur rising and falling in an uneven rhythm. Each creak of the trees outside made her pulse pound like a drum, warning of danger, danger, danger.

Wally shifted in the bunk below, signaling his own sleepless struggle. Despite his years of experience as a detective, the current investigation seemed to be taking a toll on him as well. Tammy heard his deep, steady breaths as he regulated himself, but the occasional groan revealed his true state of mind.

Mrs. Temperance lay motionless in her bunk, her rainbow shawl draped over her like a patchwork quilt. Her face appeared serene in sleep, the worry lines smoothed away. Her silver hair splayed across the pillow like a halo. Every so often, her fingers twitched as if knitting invisible yarn, her subconscious working through the day's events. A soft snore escaped her nose.

How could she sleep so soundly after the day they had? Perhaps it was a skill gained with age. The ability to compartmentalize, to set aside the worries of the day and surrender to slumber seemed like a superpower to Tammy's restless mind.

Deputy Brown's vigil outside gave some comfort.

Moonlight filtered through the thin curtains, casting silver streaks across the quilt Tammy had tucked around her legs. Lockie lay curled at her feet, a warm weight that should have been comforting. But comfort eluded her. The top bunk creaked as she shifted, the thin mattress offering little refuge from the relentless churn of her thoughts.

Images flickered behind her closed eyes—Nathan's wild, desperate expression, the crash of breaking glass, the suffocating darkness of the supply closet. Her pulse quickened as the memories pressed in, her forehead throbbing in tandem with the ache in her chest. The events of LA rushed in to join them: her once-trusted friend smugly holding Tammy's pages with Sally's name on it as though she'd written the words.

Dom breaking up with her mere weeks later proved she'd been blind to everything around her. It was then she understood why he had discouraged her from searching for the manuscript. The double blow had shattered her world.

Tammy squeezed her eyes shut, but the memories only sharpened, taunting her. *You're making the same mistakes,* her mother's voice sneered in her mind. The old refrain, echoing since childhood. *Too trusting. Too naive.*

She pressed her palms to her eyes. But it was useless. The nausea rose, and Tammy rolled onto her side, gripping the edge of the bunk. The wastebasket sat below on the floor, impossibly far away. Her stomach churned, but she clung to the solid frame of the bed, forcing deep breaths until the queasiness ebbed.

Lockie stirred, a gentle trill escaping his throat. He stretched, his green eyes opening to slits. He padded toward her before settling beside her hip. He nudged his head against her side, his purr starting as a low rumble. Tammy reached out, her fingers threading through his soft fur. His warmth seeped through her trembling hand.

Her breathing slowed, each stroke of Lockie's fur drawing her further from the edge. His unblinking gaze locked with hers, calm and steady, as if saying, "You're not alone."

The realization hit her like the torchlight from the deputy's flashlight earlier. She didn't have to face it by herself. The people of Willowcroft—Olivia, Mrs. Temperance, Wally, even Xander—had become her anchors. They'd accepted her, quirks and all, and reminded her of the connection she'd been missing of late. Mrs. Bennett's decades of fear and silence struck her anew, a cautionary tale Tammy refused to follow.

*I don't want to live like that. I won't.*

Her mind flitted to the photo of her and Sally, still packed away in an untouched box at the cottage. She saw it: two friends who had their whole lives ahead of them. That picture had been a painful reminder for months. Now, it held a different meaning—not a relic of betrayal, but a turning point. Without Sally's deception, Tammy wouldn't have left LA, wouldn't be in Willowcroft, wouldn't have stood shoulder to shoulder with her quirky new friends, solving mysteries that once only existed in her imagination. The pain lingered, but it no longer defined her.

Tammy brushed a tear from her cheek, her hand still resting on Lockie's warm side. She vowed to unpack that photo when the cottage was hers again, not to dwell on the hurt, but as a symbol of her decision to embrace the future. To trust, to connect, and let this town become her home.

They would find Nathan and get justice for Mary—that had to come first. Only then could she move back into the little blue cottage and make Willowcroft her home. But she knew now she wouldn't face it alone. She'd rebuild her writing career with the support of new friends who had already proved their worth. Her instincts were right—she'd trusted the right people. *Take that, Mother.*

The bunk creaked as she lay back down, Lockie curling into the crook of her side. She closed her eyes, letting the steady rhythm of his purring lull her to sleep.

Tammy stirred, blinking awake slowly as she took in the unfamiliar surroundings. For a moment, the events of the previous day felt hazy, like a strange dream. Then it all came rushing back—this was Wally's house. They were in hiding.

Olivia and Mrs. Temperance remained sleeping in their bunks across the room.

Beside her, Lockie stretched, his green eyes flickering as he yawned. She stroked his soft fur. "I wish you could tell me what you know about all of this." The cat stared at her, his wise gaze seeming to hold secrets beyond comprehension.

The smell of sizzling batter and syrup wafted into the room, accompanied by the clink of dishes from the kitchen. The scent transported her back to lazy Saturday mornings as a child. She peeked at the bunk below her to find Wally's bed empty.

Tammy followed her nose.

"Morning," Wally said as he flicked a pancake onto a waiting plate. His hair stood on end, giving him an almost comical appearance.

"Good morning." She ran fingers through her own tangled hair. Their tired expressions and disheveled appearances mirrored each other's restless night.

Wally poured fresh batter onto a sizzling griddle. The enticing aroma and satisfying sound filled the room, creating a homely atmosphere despite the current state of affairs.

"Thought we could all use a solid breakfast."

Tammy stretched to relieve the crick in her neck. She'd tossed and turned all night, her mind spinning with unanswered questions. "Smells delicious." She took a seat at the kitchen table. Lockie leaped onto her lap, making himself comfortable as he spied Wally with unblinking eyes.

"Thanks," Wally replied, flipping a pancake in the air.

The crackle of batter on the griddle and the fresh coffee drew the rest of the team from their beds.

Olivia shuffled in, yawning. "Is that food?"

Wally poured her a cup of coffee. Mrs. Temperance followed soon after with her fluffy slippers scuffing on the tile floor.

"Good morning, dears," she said, heading to the table. Olivia pulled out a chair for her before taking a seat herself.

"Sleep well?" Wally asked, handing over piping hot cups of coffee.

Mrs. Temperance waved a hand. "Oh, not too bad for these old bones."

Olivia smiled over the rim of her mug. "How do you do it, Mrs. Temperance? With everything going on, you're still as chipper as ever in the morning."

Mrs. Temperance chuckled. "When you get to be my age, every morning you wake up is a gift." Her expression turned serious. "But I am troubled by the events surrounding poor Nathan."

Wally took his seat again. "A sad situation all around. I fear the boy's grandfather has fed him some tall tales."

"It's a blessing no one was seriously hurt," said Olivia.

"Eat," he announced, setting a stacked plate of golden pancakes on the table. He placed some on a second plate. "I'll take these out to Brown."

Wally went outside while everyone helped themselves to pancakes and fresh orange juice. How long had he been up to get everything prepared?

As Tammy stuffed another bite of pancake into her mouth, Wally returned.

"Something that's been bothering me," he said, as he sat and helped himself, "is the locked room aspect of Mary's death. How can someone commit a murder in a room with no exit and not be caught?"

Tammy chewed before responding. "It is a puzzle. We're missing a clue." She glanced at Lockie. "Any ideas?"

Lockie tilted his head but didn't speak.

"He may be just a cat, but sometimes I feel like he knows more than he lets on."

Wally raised an eyebrow. "You might be onto something. Lockie acted strangely in your living room last night. Maybe he does know something about the locked room mystery."

"Or he was hungry," Tammy suggested as she gave Lockie some of her pancakes. But her curiosity was piqued. She stared into the cat's intelligent eyes and wondered.

"Either way," Wally continued, "we should keep an eye on him. Animals have instincts we humans can't even fathom. Lockie might lead us to the answer." He took a sip of coffee. "As soon as we get access, we'll take him to the cottage."

Tammy swiped a finger across her chin, collecting the maple syrup, then licked it clean. Did Lockie hold the answers? She wanted that knowledge now.

Olivia speared a piece of pancake. "If only Mary could tell us what happened. Séance anyone?"

"I've been turning it over and over," Wally said, ignoring Olivia's suggestion. "We have the basic sequence of events, but the how and why elude me." Wally slumped in his chair.

Mrs. Temperance reached over and gave his arm a sympathetic pat. "We'll figure it out. A thorough inspection of the cottage is in order."

"I'm itching to examine that fireplace," said Wally.

"We'll pull the fireplace apart if we have to," said Tammy.

The front door opening made everyone jump and turn in that direction. Xander entered, carrying an empty plate. "Morning! Deputy Brown said to tell you it was delicious," Xander reported.

"Good to know my culinary skills are appreciated," Wally said, taking another bite of pancake dripping in syrup.

"Xander!" Mrs. Temperance exclaimed. "What are you doing here? I thought you were at home. This has become way too dangerous for a teenager."

He tugged his backpack off and adjusted his glasses. "I couldn't sit there knowing you all were here working on the case. Besides, there's an officer outside, so it's not like I'm in danger."

"True, but you must understand our concern," Olivia said, gesturing for him to take a seat. "We want you to be safe."

"Thanks, Ms. Huddlestone," Xander replied, helping himself to a pancake. "But I'm not backing down. We're a team, right?"

"Right," Wally agreed, his gaze serious but approving. "We all need to watch each other's backs. Things may escalate."

"Understood," said Xander.

The group updated Xander about the previous night's happenings.

"Wow, that's a lot to process," he said, taking a sip of orange juice.

"Let's summarize where we're at," said Wally. "Eleanor Cross, a.k.a. Mrs. Bennett, saw someone running away from the little blue cottage the night of the murder. We now believe she lied about the description to remove her brother Max as a suspect. Nathan, we assume, has knowledge of this thanks to the ramblings of his grandfather."

Olivia dove in. "And are we assuming the bank robbery and the murder are connected?"

"Nathan's second note about the money would suggest so," Wally offered. "What if Mary knew something about the heist? Max threatened her to keep quiet, then killed her."

Olivia carried her empty plate to the dishwasher. "If we go further back, Mary's a witness and Max threatens her with the letter Tammy found in the attic." Olivia paced across the kitchen, changing direction with each point. "When she doesn't leave town, Max kills her. Eleanor sees Max running away from the cottage on the night of the murder and he makes her lie to cover it up."

"And the stolen money was never found," said Xander. "Maybe it's still hidden, and that's what Nathan was trying to learn from his grandfather's memories, where the loot is."

"And the locked room?" Wally asked.

"And no murder weapon," Xander added.

"We need the murder weapon and to find where Max hid while the officers were looking for evidence," said Tammy. "He had to be there and only later ran away, disturbing McLeod's sheep."

Lockie meowed loudly, his eyes wide and bright as he ogled Tammy. "Lockie knows something." He meowed again. "There has to be a hiding place in the living room."

"Once the cottage is no longer a crime scene, we'll go," Wally said.

"It's time my cottage gave up its secrets."

"I'll check with Brown for any updates," Wally said, as he peeked out the window. "There's a bathroom down the hall and towels in the cupboard." Wally waved in a vague direction as he headed for the front door.

A familiar surge of anticipation rose within him, a rare sensation since hanging up his badge two years ago. Retirement had its perks, but the thrill of the chase? That was difficult to replicate, until now.

Outside, Deputy Brown stood at attention. "Morning, Sheriff Wallace, sir," he said, adjusting his hat.

"Just Wally, now." Two years on and the title remained, despite the lack of privileges. "Any news on Nathan?"

"No, sir... er... Wally." He took a deep breath. "Nathan's still at large, so we'll be sticking around to keep an eye on things."

"Understandable... We were hoping to visit the little blue cottage. Still a crime scene?"

"Nope, you're good to go," Brown confirmed. "As long as you don't interfere with any ongoing investigative work, of course."

"Wouldn't dream of it," Wally assured him, a hint of his Boston accent slipping through. The familiarity of protocol and procedure brought warmth to his chest. Maybe retirement wasn't what he needed, after all. Though, working outside the lines came with advantages, too.

"I'll escort you there when you're ready."

"Excellent." *Time for some answers.*

As he walked back inside, past cases flooded his thoughts—linking clues, the satisfaction of justice served. Wally's senses sharpened. Every detail of the room came into crisp focus, from the faint scuff marks on the hardwood floor to the aroma of pancakes ghosting the air. His mind formulated theories with a speed he hadn't experienced in the last couple of years. He straightened his spine and shrugged off the sluggishness of retirement. The familiar weight of responsibility settled upon him, not as a burden, but as a friend he'd craved.

"Brown says we can go to the cottage, but he'll stick with us since Nathan is still at large."

"Good to know we have backup," Mrs. Temperance remarked.

"Let's gather our gear and head over," Wally announced. "We've got a mystery to solve. And don't forget Lockie." He glanced at the cat next to Tammy, whipping his tail like the pendulum of a grandfather clock marking the passing of time. "He knows something we don't."

"Meow."

Tammy stroked him. "Right. He'll sniff out the clues."

Olivia swept her hands back and forth across her face like a magician. She turned to the feline and, in a deep, movie trailer voice, said, "In the world of dark

alleys and hidden secrets, this cat is the undisputed king of deduction." Lockie
purred louder.

Olivia's impromptu performance lightened the mood, and Wally sniggered
along with the others.

"If Lockie is our star detective," said Mrs. Temperance, "I suppose we're his
faithful sidekicks."

"Never thought I'd be taking orders from a cat," said Xander, "but here we
are."

"No such thing as feline consultants in my day. But hey, times change," said
Wally.

As the group bustled about getting themselves together, Wally fell into old
habits. He checked his pockets for a notepad and pen. His eyes swept the room,
cataloging each person's movements, automatically coordinating their efforts. He
held the door, ushering everyone out with a, "Watch your step." The easy rhythm
of teamwork, the unspoken understanding in shared glances, the collective energy
focused on a common goal—it all washed over him like the smooth progression
of a well-solved case. *I've still got it.*

They split between the cars with Olivia, Tammy, and Lockie in Wally's car, and
Mrs. Temperance and Xander in the squad car with Brown.

# Chapter 23

As Deputy Brown led the team along the road to the little blue cottage, the scent of pine needles wafted through the open windows. Tammy's knees jerked up and down. Her eyes flicked between her friends and the passing scenery. What awaited them inside her home? Her writer's mind crafted multiple scenarios. Were they reaching the climax or a red herring?

The two vehicles stopped outside the cottage's cheery exterior belying the potential darkness within. The officer stepped out, hand on his holster. "Stay put," he commanded. "I'll secure the scene."

Tammy gripped the door handle.

"Relax," Olivia said, placing a reassuring hand on her shoulder. "We're safe with Deputy Brown and Detective Wallace." She gave a mock salute in Wally's direction.

"Right," Tammy said, releasing the door handle. The deputy entered her house. This was it. Years of mystery might be laid to rest. Or, a small voice sounding suspiciously like her mother, whispered she could be making a fool of herself. She tried to shake the thought away.

Her gaze fell onto Lockie perched on the dashboard, alert and twitching.

The front door flung open. A figure appeared. Nathan! His face twisted in panic.

"Freeze!" Deputy Brown barked, his firearm drawn and aimed at Nathan. "Hands above your head!"

Tammy squealed. Olivia sat forward, trying to get a better view.

Nathan let out an animalistic howl as he lunged at the officer. The two men collided with a noisy scuffle. Nathan wiggled free and sprinted behind the cottage.

"Stay there!" the officer shouted to them as he gave chase.

Tammy's hands clutched the edge of her seat. What was he doing inside her home?

*Please catch him.*

"Look," Olivia said, gesturing toward the field.

Two silhouettes swished through the tall grass, Nathan and the deputy heading away from the cottage.

Tammy's heart pounded in her chest, the rapid beats mirroring the urgency of the situation. She exchanged glances with Wally and Olivia, and with Xander who was looking through the rear window of the squad car in front. Without words, they all shared a mutual understanding of what needed to be done next.

Olivia leaned into the front seat. "Let's do this. We need to find out what Nathan was doing inside."

The forms disappeared. Tammy turned to Wally. "Now's our chance."

Wally nodded. They exited the car, collected Xander and Mrs. Temperance from the squad car, and hurried up the porch steps. The front door sat ajar from Nathan's exit. Tammy paused. It had all started here seventy years ago.

Tammy stepped over the threshold. The living room, bathed in the soft glow of morning light, looked undisturbed apart from the broken glass.

"Where's your broom, dear?" Mrs. Temperance asked.

Tammy gestured to the other side of the fireplace. "In the kitchen."

"I'll get it, Mrs. Temperance," Olivia said. "You keep a watch for Nathan and Deputy Brown, in case they come back." She left the room while Mrs. Temperance approached the window to keep guard.

Tammy scanned the room. "Where do we start?" The task of discovering what Nathan was up to was daunting.

A brush against her leg made her look down. Of course—her furry partner would know where to begin. She followed as Lockie padded toward the fireplace. She scrutinized the brickwork, then recalled an overlooked clue.

"The fireplace," she said aloud, startling Olivia as she returned with a dustpan and broom. "Xander, remember the newspaper article about renovations?"

"Of course," Xander replied, pulling out his phone to find his digital murder board. "Guys, listen to this. In 1953, the 'old hearth' was replaced by a smaller modern fireplace, with the *Cross* Construction Company handling the project."

A spark ignited inside Tammy. Lockie scratched at the bricks near the fireplace's edge. "Lockie knew all along." The clever cat focused on the left side. "That's where we need to search."

Tammy's brain kicked into gear. "Max wasn't in the 1954 yearbook, so he'd be around nineteen or older at the time of the murder. Maybe he worked on the renovation with his dad's construction company, meaning he'd know the house." She rapped her knuckles against the fireplace's façade. "Could it be hollow between the bookshelf and the fireplace?"

Wally's eyebrows shot up. "Let me see if I can find a loose stone or something."

"Is there enough space?" Xander asked.

"We'll soon find out." Wally reached for the poker. He tapped its metal tip on the edge of the hearth, focusing where Lockie had shown interest. Everything seemed secure, but Tammy buzzed at the idea of a concealed nook.

She crouched beside Wally. The world narrowed to just the fireplace. Did it hold the key to unraveling the mystery? She followed Wally's every move, eager to assist at the slightest indication. The thought of potential clues dried her mouth, while the lingering hint of soot and faint scent of charred wood filled her senses. Thank goodness it was summer. Hot ash would make a messy complication.

Wally crawled inside the fireplace. "The stones are smooth and rounded. One large boulder is flanked by smaller ones in each corner." He prodded a small one. "I've got subtle movement here!" He pushed again. Tammy's vision blurred with rapid blinks, but there was no denying it—it shifted. Lockie let out a meow of approval.

Olivia moved next to Tammy who could almost feel Olivia's curiosity bubbling over like a volcano ready to erupt. *She's even more curious than I am—if that's possible.*

"Pass me the log grabber."

Olivia handed the tool over. *How would I know what a log grabber was?* It had ends like dragon talons ready to snatch secrets from their hiding place. Tammy's writer's mind was in full swing.

Wally maneuvered the tool around the shifted stone, making a scraping sound. His face scrunched in concentration, reminding her of a detective from one of her books on the brink of a breakthrough.

With a gentle pull, it yielded. "If I remove the four smaller ones, we should be able to grip the larger one and move it aside."

Tammy's imagination zoomed ahead to what lay in the secret nook. A hidden treasure? More letters? Evidence of murder? Each would make the perfect climax of a well-crafted story. She wanted to flip to the last page to discover the ending.

Wally pried the small ones free. Dust and debris showered down. "Now for the big one."

His hands splayed across the boulder's rough surface. He grunted, muscles straining, face contorting with effort.

"Move!"

It yielded, rolling with the dramatic flair of an adventure novel. Tammy stumbled backward as the stone missed her toes by mere inches. The visceral danger sent a tremor through her body. But then she realized it was only a slice of a boulder, meaning there would be unaccounted-for space between the fireplace wall and where the bookshelves started.

Lockie dashed into the revealed area.

Tammy followed Lockie into the fireplace as her anticipation mounted. The cool air from the cavity crossed her face; it was musty and stale. Her fingers brushed against the rough edges. There was just enough room for someone to squeeze inside if they were desperate enough. Spider webs and dust filled the corners, undisturbed for decades.

Lockie poked his head out and meowed, as if to say, 'I told you so.' He'd known all along. Her heart swelled with admiration for her clever cat. But reluctant to pat him while covered in cobwebs.

"Max could've hidden in here after the murder until everyone left the crime scene." Tammy said. Did the hollow solve the locked room part of the mystery?

"Wow," Mrs. Temperance said, having left her lookout post to inspect for herself. "That's a tight fit."

Tammy shined her phone's flashlight into the cubbyhole. There was something wedged against the wall, reflecting light from the torch. "There's something here!" Her hands tried to pry it loose.

"Here, let me try," Olivia offered. She freed the object and brought it into the daylight. "Umm, guys." Her hand shook as she held up her discovery—a knife with the blade stained with dark splotches.

A collective gasp was audible.

"The murder weapon?" Olivia asked.

Tammy was dumbfounded. After all these years, they'd found it, hidden inside the fireplace of *her* cottage. Goosebumps broke out across her body at the thought of sharing her living room with a murder weapon.

Lockie hissed and swiped at the air.

"Really?" gasped Xander.

Tammy couldn't take her eyes off it. "Wow..." The encrusted blood was a chilling reminder of the crime.

"Put it down," Wally commanded. "We don't want to tamper with evidence."

"We should get this to Deputy Brown," said Xander.

"He's a little busy right now," said Mrs. Temperance.

Olivia turned the knife over in her hands. "A modern lab could test for DNA and fingerprints and confirm if Max Cross was the killer."

A commotion outside grabbed Tammy's attention. She hurried to the window. "He's caught Nathan!"

Relief washed over her. Nathan was in custody; they were safe.

"He's cuffing him and putting him into the squad car."

Nathan twisted in Deputy Brown's grip, turning back toward the cottage. His gaze locked with Tammy's—icy and unforgiving, making her shudder. As he struggled, his hoodie slipped down his arms, revealing a bright blue T-shirt. Her eyes widened at the familiar color and the pixelated shape of a wide-eyed ghost. Was that what Marjorie had seen? As he turned, she caught sight of a bold yellow circle with a wedge missing, emblazoned on the back.

*The arcade-themed T-shirt... the ghost design T-shirt... It's the same person! Nathan was the one outside my cottage the day I found the letter, and the one who nearly ran over Marjorie.* The pieces clicked into place. *He's been involved before we were.*

"This was supposed to be mine! All mine!" Nathan yelled as the deputy wrangled him into the car. His accusatory tone and venomous eyes rattled Tammy. "This isn't over."

Tammy recoiled from the window.

"None of this belongs to you."

What was she missing? His unwavering certainty made her feel like a novel's protagonist who'd overlooked a crucial clue.

Lockie flicked his tail around her legs.

The deputy shoved Nathan into the squad car. Tammy flinched as the door slammed shut.

Wally put a hand on her shoulder, causing her to jump. "He can't hurt you now."

# Chapter 24

Sirens sounded in Tammy's ears.

"Brown's backup," Wally said, as a second squad car screeched to a halt outside.

"It's Sheriff Stanton and another deputy," Tammy said as she turned to the middle of the room where Olivia still gripped the knife. The sight brought anxiety and relief.

She crouched by Lockie. "We're one step closer to solving this, aren't we, boy?" The cat blinked at her.

The officers entered the living room, spotting the weapon.

"Where did you find that?" Sheriff Stanton said, darting between the knife and Wally.

"Hey, Stanton. We found something! It was concealed beside the fireplace," Wally said, gesturing to the now-exposed compartment.

Stanton's gaze shifted to the secret space, a blend of admiration and concern on his face. He put on a pair of latex gloves. "Let me take that from you."

"Of course," Olivia replied, surrendering the knife.

"This is evidence now," he declared while placing it into an official bag held by the second deputy. He sealed the bag with precision. "Where exactly did you find it?"

"Behind the fireplace, sir." Xander pointed to the boulder perched on the floor. Lockie rubbed against the opening, guiding Stanton's attention.

"I read the Mary Collins disheveled case file last night." The sheriff glared at Wally, who shrugged and averted his eyes. "A locked room murder, huh?" Stanton peered into the hole.

"We think the killer hid in there until everyone left the crime scene," Olivia offered.

"And he ran across the field late at night, disturbing Reginald McLeod and his sheep," Tammy added.

"Interesting," said Stanton, as he surveyed the space. "Brown said he found Nathan inspecting the fireplace when he arrived. We'll get forensics to analyze the knife. In the meantime, we're going to search this cottage thoroughly."

How had her sanctuary become a crime scene twice in two days? Her LA apartment had never been a backdrop for a mystery in all her years there. Was this house concealing more secrets?

Tammy and her friends clustered near the window. The officers moved systematically around her living room, their flashlights illuminating every corner and crevice. One knelt beside the fireplace, running a gloved hand along the inside of the hidden compartment, while another dusted for fingerprints. Their muffled conversations were punctuated by the occasional radio crackle.

Was it right or wrong that Tammy cataloged the men's movements for improved authenticity for future books?

"Look at them," Olivia said, her eyes locked on the deputies. "They're so methodical."

"Every little detail counts," Wally said. "We're close, but we need solid proof against Max."

"Are you okay, Tammy?" Olivia asked, placing a reassuring hand on her friend's arm. "This must be overwhelming to see in your own house."

"Tell me about it." She forced a weak smile. Writing about it was easy compared to this. "But at least we're getting closer to the truth." *Am I ready for the truth?* She hugged herself and braced for whatever might surface.

"Yes," Mrs. Temperance agreed, her gaze fixed on the bustling deputies. "I never thought we'd uncover something like this."

"Me neither," said Xander. "This is definitely one for the history books."

"Quite literally," Olivia quipped, laughing at her own joke.

The officers moved to the kitchen. Too restless to stay still, her feet carried her in a slow circle around the living room. The room felt different now—lighter, its secrets revealed.

She paused to peer into the fireplace. *Imagine crouching in there, heart pounding, while people searched for you mere inches away.*

"It had to have been Max, right?" Xander said. "He argued with Mary about not leaving town and killed her."

"It's plausible he knew about the nook if he'd worked on the fireplace renovations," Tammy offered.

Wally nodded. "Absolutely."

"They argued about the heist and he stabbed Mary in a fit of rage," Olivia said, imitating stabbing actions.

"Then Victor knocked on the door," Tammy said.

"Max locked it from the inside, leaving the key in the lock, to buy time and hid in the compartment," added Xander.

"Leaving poor Mary's body there alone. Her murder unsolved all these years," Olivia said, shaking her head.

"And after everyone had gone, he slipped out, leaving the weapon behind," said Mrs. Temperance.

Tammy halted mid-step. "We're finally piecing it together." Were they ready for the truth? No matter what it was?

Lockie purred. She stroked his back, taking comfort in his softness.

"But how did Nathan know to come to the cottage?" Olivia asked.

Wally tapped his chin thoughtfully. "Good point. Max must have mentioned it in his rambles. We need to find out more about him."

"Are you suggesting we talk to him?" Xander asked, his grip tightening on the back of a nearby chair. "That would be interesting."

Tammy's stomach knotted. *Was she going to talk to a murderer?*

"But his dementia is pretty advanced," said Mrs. Temperance.

"It can't hurt to try," Olivia said, her eyes darting from one face to another.

"Agreed," Wally said.

"The audacity of sneaking out late at night and leaving the knife behind…" Mrs. Temperance said.

"Maybe he thought if they hadn't found him hiding in there, they'd never locate the murder weapon, so best to leave it," Wally suggested.

The hours blurred as Tammy and her friends underwent a series of interviews. Questions overlapped, each officer seeking clarity on the unfolding mystery. With the repeated recounts, her voice grew hoarse.

As the afternoon sunlight waned, the deputies packed their equipment. The once-bustling cottage grew quieter.

"We're clearing out for now," said Sheriff Stanton to Tammy. "But we'll keep your cottage as an active crime scene while we process the new evidence."

She managed a faint nod, her body heavy with exhaustion. A dull ache pulsed behind her eyes, and every muscle protested as she shifted her weight. The emotional toll of the day weighed on her—fear, exhilaration, uncertainty: all intertwining in a tangled web that left her feeling spent.

Wally stepped up and laid a hand on Tammy's shoulder. "Why don't you come stay with me again tonight?" he suggested kindly.

"That would be perfect, thanks."

"You too, Olivia, with your shop front window still broken." He turned to the others. "Mrs. Temperance and Xander, I'll take you home."

As the officers departed, their footsteps fading, Tammy stood in the doorway of her cottage. She gazed around the room—books pulled from shelves, cushions askew, the hearth bearing marks of their discovery. A lump formed in her throat. So much for a sanctuary. At least Nathan was behind bars now; the immediate threat was quelled. But the unsettling sense of invasion lingered. Would she ever get to settle into what was supposed to be her cozy retreat?

"Come on, Lockie," she called to the cat. "We're staying with Wally again tonight."

Lockie trotted after her, his gentle padding a comforting presence amidst the uncertainty. Everyone followed Wally to his car, and Tammy closed the door.

"Thanks for letting me stay," Tammy said as she ate the last bite of the grilled cheese Wally had made for them all.

"Of course. You're always welcome here." He looked at Olivia. "All of you."

Olivia smiled as she stacked the dishwasher.

Tammy perched on the edge of the sofa, one hand stroking Lockie's soft fur, while the other pressed the tender bulge on her forehead, wincing at the pain.

Olivia gestured in Tammy's direction. "Since last night, your bump's sprouted colors like one of Mrs. Temperance's shawls."

"I'm just glad we stopped Nathan before he hurt Mrs. Bennett or anyone else." *But we have more to uncover.* "We should go see Max and Mrs. Bennett first thing in the morning. Between the two of them, they know what happened."

Wally handed Tammy some ibuprofen. "That's the next logical step."

Olivia appeared troubled. "I wish I could come with you, but I have to sort out the bookstore—fix the broken window and make sure it's secure."

Tammy swallowed the pain relief. "Absolutely." She reached out to give Olivia's hand a gentle squeeze. "You take care of what you need to do. Wally and I can handle the nursing home visit."

"I feel like I'm abandoning you."

"You're not," Tammy assured her. "We're in this together, no matter where we are."

"We'll collect Mrs. Temperance on the way," Wally said. "I'm sure she'd want to check if Mrs. Bennett has returned from the hospital."

Tammy's eyes lit up at the suggestion. "Of course, Mrs. Temperance must come. She's built a good relationship with Mrs. Bennett."

"We're so close to the truth," Olivia said.

"Agreed," Wally replied. "But for now, let's get some rest. It's been a big day."

Lockie stretched languidly and hopped off the sofa. He padded across the room. "Lockie is ready for sleep," said Tammy.

"Me too," said Olivia.

With a plan in place for the morning, they headed to bed.

In the guest room, Tammy slipped into her pajamas left from the night before. She climbed into bed, the sheets cool against her skin. As she stared at the ceiling, images flooded her mind—the glint of the knife, Nathan's cold stare, the hidden nook in her fireplace. She turned onto her side, pulling the blanket over her chin.

# Chapter 25

Wally stepped into Serenity Gardens with Tammy, Mrs. Temperance, and Lockie behind him. His nose wrinkled at the bleach smell permeating from every surface, taking him back to countless crime scenes where perps had tried to destroy evidence. In his day on the force, he'd visited plenty of places like this. They never got any cheerier. A young nurse hurried past them, her rubber-soled shoes squeaking like a mouse on the run. The absence of a welcoming committee left them to navigate their own path to check on Mrs. Bennett. They strode down the hall. Lockie led the way.

The cat stopped outside one of the doors, tail flicking.

"Here we are," Mrs. Temperance announced.

Tammy knocked on the door. Last time she was here, Nathan had given her the kaleidoscopic tennis ball residing on her forehead. Tough as nails, she hadn't complained about it once.

Tammy creaked the door ajar, and they all entered. Wally's trained eye swept over the room. A single bed, a nightstand—nothing more. *Places like this stripped life to the bone.* He shuddered inwardly. *Please don't let me end my days here.*

A slight frame lay swaddled in blankets, her eyes closed.

"Mrs. Bennett?" Tammy called out as they approached the bed. The elderly woman's eyes fluttered open, revealing a glimmer of recognition as she focused on the women.

"Tammy... and Hazel." Her voice was weak.

"Hello, Eleanor," Mrs. Temperance said.

Wally stood back so as not to impose. Besides, he had other residents to visit. But he also wanted an update on her condition.

Tammy placed a hand on Mrs. Bennett's arm. "Are you feeling better? We were so concerned after last night."

"Thank you," she replied. "I'm glad to be back home, at least."

Home. That word felt wrong in reference to the antiseptic prison. But Tammy said, "Good."

Mrs. Temperance took the one chair, leaving Tammy to stand. Lockie settled by the window, keeping watch.

"Now," said Tammy, "we understand this will be difficult, but we need your help. It's important we uncover the truth about what happened all those years ago—both the robbery and Mary's murder."

Mrs. Temperance sat tall. "Please, Eleanor, tell us everything you remember."

Mrs. Bennett's fingers fumbled for the glass on the nightstand, and Wally tensed. He was too far away to catch it if it fell. The water sloshed close to the rim as she raised it to her lips. She closed her eyes and emptied the glass.

With the women settled, he slipped away to seek out Max. He wanted it finished so he could leave the depressing place.

Stanton and a couple of deputies were talking with a nurse at the front desk. *Dang. They got to Max first.* He shoved his hands in his pockets, hoping to hide his frustration.

The sheriff caught him. "Wally."

"Stanton." He gave a nod of acknowledgment. "What brings you here?"

"Max Cross. We were here to question him about the murder and request DNA and fingerprint samples. But we've received unfortunate news."

"What?" Wally's guts tightened as he waited for the punchline.

"Max Cross passed away early this morning."

Wally's jaw dropped. "Well, I'll be." Max Cross dead? Fortuitous timing. He slumped. How much truth had died with him? Wally forced himself to refocus. "Did you get any forensics from the knife?" After seventy years, it was a long shot.

Stanton glanced around before answering. "Results aren't back, but the lab found skin cells and fingerprints."

"Finally, some solid evidence." Would it confirm Max was the murderer? He placed a grateful hand on the sheriff's shoulder. "I know some folks who will want to hear about this."

Wally turned on his heel and headed back to Mrs. Bennett's room, the weight of Max's death heavy in his soul. But progress had been made—the knife and the DNA. With her brother dead and her nephew behind bars for attempted murder, it was time for her to tell the truth.

He buried his excitement to focus on the sad news he had to convey.

"I'm sorry, ladies, but Max died this morning," Wally said, steady but somber. He studied Mrs. Bennett's reaction.

"They informed me earlier," she said, her voice barely above a whisper. The sterile walls of the nursing home seemed to close in, quiet settling over the room.

Tammy moved closer to Mrs. Bennett. "I'm sorry for your loss."

"Condolences, my dear," Mrs. Temperance added.

The tension eased from Mrs. Bennett's body, her petite frame straightened as if lighter. The air in the room lightened, a subtle yet tangible change.

"Ladies, I have a second update I think you'll want to hear," Wally announced, unable to keep the information to himself any longer.

All eyes focused on him. "They found DNA and fingerprints on the knife." He'd never wanted DNA results more in his whole career.

"This changes everything," Mrs. Temperance said. "It should provide physical proof that Max committed the crimes."

Mrs. Bennett stared ahead, with no obvious reaction to the news.

Tammy reached out and grasped her hand. "Mrs. Bennett? Did you hear what Wally said about the evidence?"

Of course, this news would hit her the hardest. Max was her brother.

"We know you and Max had a complicated history," Tammy said. "But he was still family. If you need to talk or want company, we're here."

Mrs. Bennett offered a sad smile, patting Tammy's hand. She took a deep breath. "It's time for the truth."

Lockie leaped onto the bed, settling next to Mrs. Bennett with a purr. *That cat knows how to read a room.*

The woman's eyes flickered with surprise and then softened as she turned her gaze toward Lockie. She extended a trembling hand to stroke him. "Well, hello there, little furry friend."

"Meet Pawlock Holmes, or Lockie," said Tammy.

Wally took the lead. "If you're ready, Mrs. Bennett, I can get Sheriff Stanton. He's just down the hall."

She gave a small nod.

Wally looked straight into her eyes before leaving. "You're very brave."

When he reached the nurse's station, he beckoned Stanton to follow him. "I have a witness for you."

"Who?"

"Max Cross's sister, Mrs. Bennett. She knows things about the night of Mary Collins's murder."

Without hesitation, Stanton followed. Wally made introductions, and Stanton wasted no time pulling out his notepad.

"Mrs. Bennett," the sheriff began, gentle but firm, "are you comfortable telling us what you know about the murder?"

Her eyes darted between Wally, Tammy, and Mrs. Temperance. Her hands fluttered in her lap, and he could see the weight of decades pressing down on her. She took a shaky breath, and when she spoke, her voice quavered.

"I've carried this secret for so long," she said. "It's eaten away at me, day after day, year after year."

A bulge formed in Wally's throat. He'd expected facts, but the raw emotion from Mrs. Bennett caught him off guard, like a sucker punch.

"Max was always a bully," she continued, growing stronger, "even when we were children." Her eyes welled with tears. "He was so tall, but he forced me to say I'd seen a short man. That was the lie that helped him get away with murder."

Wally's fists clenched as anger simmered beneath his skin.

Her gaze drifted to the paintings adorning the walls of her room. Mrs. Temperance followed her line of sight. "Your artwork brings so much life to this place, Eleanor. It's hard to believe these are all yours."

A wistful expression crossed Mrs. Bennett's face. "Not all of them." She gestured toward a landscape painting opposite her bed. "That one... is Mary's."

Wally's breath caught as he stared at the painting, his throat tightening. Each delicate brush stroke made by Mary's own hand, a fragment of her soul preserved before violence stole her future. Seventy years dissolved in an instant.

"Mary and I were friends," Mrs. Bennett explained, her face soft with nostalgia. "She taught me to paint when I was a young teen. She saw something in me that I couldn't see in myself." Her fingers traced invisible patterns on her bedspread. "After... after she died, I used all my pocket money savings to buy that painting at her estate sale. I wanted something of hers."

Mrs. Temperance squeezed Mrs. Bennett's hand. "A beautiful gesture."

Mrs. Bennett's eyes never left the painting. "The town was so focused on the bank heist... Mary got overlooked in all the chaos. But I didn't want her to be forgotten completely. I've kept this painting close all these years, hoping someday I'd find a way to get Mary the justice she deserved.

"That night... I saw my brother at Mary's cottage." Mrs. Bennett's gaze grew distant. "Later, I heard Mary had been killed. I knew it must have been Max." A sob escaped her lips. "He-he threatened me. Said if I didn't help him, he would make sure I regretted it. I've lived in fear for so long, always looking over my shoulder, wondering if today would be the day he'd make good on his threat. And then came Nathan."

Tammy reached out, placing a hand on Mrs. Bennett's arm. "You did what you had to do to stay safe. Neither Max nor Nathan can hurt you anymore."

Mrs. Bennett's tears spilled over. "I should have come forward sooner, but I was scared. Can you ever forgive me?"

Mrs. Temperance enveloped Mrs. Bennett's hands in her own. "You're doing the right thing now. That's what matters."

Wally respected the elderly woman, recognizing the burden she'd carried all these years.

With a deep, shivering breath, she continued her account of that fateful night. "It was Max I saw running from Mary's cottage."

Wally's heart pounded. *This is it. We're going to find out what those poor officers in 1954 never knew.*

"I got up late to use the bathroom, and his light was on. I saw his shadow under the door, pacing. I pressed my ear closer and heard him mumbling about money and murder." She turned to Mrs. Temperance. "He always mumbled... even before the dementia.

"The next day, when I learned about Mary's death, it all fell into place. Max must have been involved with the bank heist. I think Mary discovered something she shouldn't have... So Max killed her to keep her quiet."

Wally saw the mix of relief and anguish on Mrs. Bennett's face. She'd finally unburdened herself, but her brother's actions still pressed heavily upon her.

"He was my brother," she said, her voice breaking. "I wanted to love him. But what he did... I can't protect him anymore."

Mrs. Bennett's gaze returned to Mary's painting. "I thought about telling the truth a thousand times... but every time I opened my mouth, fear would close it." She shook her head, tears welling again. "And now Nathan's life is ruined too."

Tammy placed a hand on Mrs. Bennett's arm. "You were scared. They threatened you."

"I know, but..." she trailed off, lost in memories. "I married young. Moved to Lakeview. It gave me some distance from Max, allowed me to breathe easier." She let out a bitter laugh. "But it all came rushing back when we ended up in the same nursing home."

Wally's brow furrowed. "That must have been terrifying for you."

"Yes. But Max's dementia... it made him less intimidating. An old man mumbling to himself." Her expression darkened. "But then Nathan started asking questions."

"Nathan from last night?" Stanton asked, his pen poised over his notepad.

"Yes. Max's grandson. My great-nephew," Mrs. Bennett explained. "He became quite aggressive, demanding I tell him what happened back then. It was like being fifteen again, with Max threatening me. Nathan is so much like his grandfather."

She turned to Mrs. Temperance. "After your first visit, he told me he could get to me anytime he wanted."

The hairs on the back of Wally's neck stood on end. "What was Nathan after?"

Mrs. Bennett sighed. "The money. He thought Max had hidden it somewhere. But I didn't know anything about it, and Max never acted well off. I wondered if guilt kept him from spending it."

"And Nathan thought he'd find it based on Max's ramblings?" Tammy asked.

"Yes, but he also understood pursuing it openly could get his grandfather in trouble. He didn't want to lose access to Max before he found the money."

Stanton jotted more notes. "Mrs. Bennett, thank you for sharing all this. I know it wasn't easy."

Her shoulders sagged, her movements slow and heavy. "I hope it helps bring Mary some closure after all these years."

Wally exchanged a meaningful glance with Stanton. The pieces were connecting, but at what cost? He cleared his throat, signaling to Tammy and Mrs. Temperance. "We'll give you some privacy with Sheriff Stanton."

The trio stepped out of the room and into the sterile corridor, Wally closing the door behind them.

Tammy propped herself against the wall, her face pale. "I can't believe it. All these years..."

Mrs. Temperance shook her head, her usual composure slipping. "That poor woman, carrying such a burden for so long."

A sense of unease settled in Wally's stomach. "So many lives have been affected, and so much pain."

Tammy's eyes glistened with unshed tears. "And now what? We've opened deep wounds. Mrs. Bennett will have to live with the fact that she told the truth, but it's too late."

"And Nathan," Mrs. Temperance added. "What will happen to him now?"

Wally sighed. "I don't know."

"We should take a moment to process all this before we decide what to do next," said Tammy.

Wally appreciated the suggestion. "Let's step outside."

They made their way through the nursing home, the polished floors reflecting the fluorescent lights overhead. Bleach lingered everywhere. What secrets had it washed away?

They found a bench in the garden. The fresh air helped to clear Wally's head, but the weight of Mrs. Bennett's confession still pressed heavily on his mind. "How fragile is the past? One moment, one decision can have consequences lasting generations."

Tammy nodded. "But now everyone will know what happened and Mary will never be forgotten again."

After a few minutes of quiet reflection, Wally straightened his posture. "We need to tell Olivia and Xander."

The others agreed, and they walked to Wally's car. As they climbed in, Lockie settled on Tammy's lap, seeming to sense the somber mood.

As they pulled away, Tammy said, "I can't believe Max bullied his own sister into lying for decades."

Mrs. Temperance shook her head. "A cruel man. And poor Nathan's become a victim of Max's choices."

Wally's hands tightened on the steering wheel. "Nathan made his own decisions."

# Chapter 26

As they pulled up outside the bookstore, a glazier moved with practiced ease, installing a new pane of glass. Tammy strode through the door. The bells jingled to announce their arrival. Wally, Mrs. Temperance, and Lockie followed. Was this the climax of their real-life novel? The big reveal?

"We're here!" Tammy called out, scanning the room for Olivia or Xander, itching to share their news.

Olivia popped up from behind the counter. "You're here! We've been waiting all morning."

Xander's head appeared from between two towering bookshelves, sporting an expectant grin. "Did you discover anything? Did you?"

"We did," Tammy replied, unsure which of her mixed emotions to display.

"Come on, I have iced tea and snacks ready for us in the back room. Let's go." She led the way through the stacks toward their secret lair. Lockie trotted alongside. Tammy's stomach growled at the mention of snacks. The revelations of the morning had, until now, kept her appetite at bay.

In their little sanctuary, Olivia poured chilled drinks. The clinking of ice cubes against the glasses was a soothing sound. Tammy sipped the iced tea, the coolness calming her nerves. A chocolate chip cookie helped even more.

"Now, spill," Olivia said. "What happened at the nursing home?"

"Max passed away overnight," Wally said.

Xander's eyes widened. "Oh, no."

If only they'd visited him one day earlier. Tammy swallowed the lump in her throat with another cookie bite. "But that allowed Mrs. Bennett to talk. She told us everything she knew."

"Looks like Max killed Mary," Wally said.

"He forced Eleanor to lie for him," Mrs. Temperance said, "carrying that burden for the rest of her life."

Lockie's ears twitched; even he understood the gravity of Eleanor's torment. He leaped from his perch to curl up next to Mrs. Temperance, and she stroked his soft fur, grateful for his calming presence.

"Mrs. Bennett believes Max was involved with the heist," Wally added. "Mary must've seen something she wasn't supposed to, so Max silenced her."

They let the information sink in with expressions of disbelief, relief, and grief. Outside, leaves stirred in the wind.

Xander gripped the table edge hard enough to pale his knuckles. "Max robbed the bank, murdered Mary, and got away with it for seventy years. And now we've uncovered the truth?"

Max's life of crime hovered around Tammy like a gaping plot hole.

"Mrs. Bennett carried this secret for so long," Wally said. "Though Max took the exact details to his grave, we cracked it."

Xander leaped forward, jubilant. "We solved a locked room mystery and caught a murdering bank robber!"

Wally rubbed the back of his neck. "Who knows how this town was affected by Mary's murder? Folks must've been terrified."

Mrs. Temperance nodded. "I was too young to remember, but my parents must have lived through it... I wonder if they lost money?"

Xander flicked his screen toward her. "It's okay, Mrs. Temperance, the bank's insurance paid out."

"That's a relief," said Mrs. Temperance.

"Max's dementia was karma in the end—he gave himself away," Olivia said.

"At least the truth is out now," Tammy said.

Olivia flashed animated eyes. "And it all started with Tammy discovering a letter. We make a good team."

Tammy leaned back, letting the weight of the last few days settle in. She came seeking peace—a quiet escape from the chaos of LA and the betrayal. Instead, she stumbled into a tangled mystery.

Her fingers traced the tender bump on her forehead, a reminder of how dangerous Nathan had proved to be. If she'd tackled this alone, she might have been another victim in Max Cross's twisted legacy. Yet, here she was, surrounded by unexpected friendships that had become her lifeline. Willowcroft had given her more than a fresh start—it had shown her that the most incredible stories happen when you open yourself up to others. Her ability to trust in herself and others was restored.

Looking back, her broken Los Angeles life was a catalyst for something better. While Tammy traveled for author events and research trips, her best friend and boyfriend had been weaving their own twisted plot in her apartment. Sally had stumbled upon the final draft during a visit with Dom—visits that had nothing to do with friendship and everything to do with deceit. She snatched the manuscript and passed it off as her own. Even after Dom ended their relationship weeks later, she hadn't connected the dots. Her supposed best friend and the man she'd loved had orchestrated the perfect crime, stealing not just her heart but the best work she'd ever written. No wonder she'd lost faith in people, including herself.

Tammy raised her glass. "To new beginnings and teamwork."

Glasses clinked, and laughter broke through the remaining tension.

"I couldn't have done this without each of you."

Xander grinned. "We worked together."

Mrs. Temperance patted Tammy's hand. "You were the driving force, my dear. Your curiosity inspired us all."

Tammy ducked her head at the compliment. Then her mother wormed her way in, "Don't let it go to your head. You were just lucky." She pushed it away. *No, this was the result of the team's hard work and trust in each other.*

"And don't forget," Mrs. Temperance added, "it was Max's ramblings that led his grandson Nathan to search for the money."

"It doesn't seem fair," said Olivia, shaking her head. "Max lived a full life, while his grandson pays the price."

Mrs. Temperance helped herself to a cookie. "Nathan made his own decisions."

"Oh, when you were at the nursing home," Olivia said, "I researched further into Mary's family in the hope of finding a next of kin."

"And?" said Tammy. Providing closure to family would be so satisfying.

Olivia's face dropped. "There is none. She was an only child, no kids. Her parents were only children and they, along with her grandmother, are long gone."

"That's why the investigation faded over time," Wally said. "No one left to fight for answers."

"That's awful," Tammy said.

"But we got *Mary* justice," said Xander. "Isn't that the point?"

Mrs. Temperance squeezed his hand. "Yes, dear. That is the point."

"Even if it took a roundabout way." Olivia's voice drifted into a distant hum as fragments about Cross Construction's move to Stonefield floated past.

Mrs. Temperance's sigh cut through the fog. "It's sad when names die out. I'm the last Temperance in town, you know."

A heaviness settled over her until a blur of black and white leaped onto the table. Lockie batted at a stray cookie, pushing it this way and that. A bubble of laughter escaped from Tammy as Olivia exclaimed, "Well, I guess Lockie has decided we've been serious long enough!"

Tammy's giggles intensified, the week's tension dissolving as everyone joined in.

Even Mrs. Temperance dabbed at her eyes, shoulders shaking. "Oh my, I haven't laughed like that in ages."

Tammy's fingers found Lockie's favorite spot behind his ears. "We've accomplished something incredible here."

Mrs. Temperance's eyes twinkled. "We certainly have."

"I came for a quaint cottage and gained so much more. We may not have given closure to any relatives, but we honored Mary's memory with the truth."

"And Mrs. Bennett can finally live without that burden," Olivia said, her face brightening.

"Plus, we solved a locked room mystery!" Xander bounced in his seat. "How many people can say they've done that?"

Mrs. Temperance chuckled. "Not many. Quite the adventure we've had. And all from a letter in an attic."

"A highlight of my career," Wally added, settling back.

Warmth spread through Tammy's chest as she inspected her new friends' faces—Olivia with her genealogy passion, Mrs. Temperance's wealth of local contacts, Wally's detective instincts, Xander's tech wizardry, and Lockie, the unexpected hero.

Tammy raised a glass. "To solving mysteries and forging friendships." *See, Mother? I can make friends. I can do things right. I'm not listening to you anymore.*

"Cheers to that!" Glass clinked against glass.

"Don't forget Lockie," Xander said, sneaking him a cookie. "Our celebrity sleuth!"

Lockie's answering purr drew fresh laughter.

# Chapter 27

Tammy sipped her iced tea as the laughter died down. *Have we truly uncovered everything?*

She stood and walked to the murder board, studying their evidence.

"What's up, Tammy?" asked Olivia. "Are there some loose ends?"

"I don't think so, but should we talk it through just in case?"

"Ooh, like an Agatha Christie reveal scene," said Olivia, bouncing on her toes.

"It can't hurt," agreed Mrs. Temperance.

"Let's examine the facts," Wally said, folding his shirt sleeves. "It started with Max Cross. Advanced dementia or not, he remembered more than anyone understood."

Olivia nodded. "Nathan visited him regularly. And Max began mumbling."

Wally sat forward. "Two or three words here and there. Random at first glance."

Xander drummed his fingers on the table. "We're assuming Max said words like bank heist and the little blue cottage."

As Mrs. Temperance started a fresh pot of coffee with Olivia, she said, "Nathan did what anyone might do—he researched. He discovered the murder of Mary Collins and made assumptions about his grandfather's involvement."

"He wanted to protect his grandfather," Tammy said, returning to her chair. "But there was more to it than that."

Olivia rubbed her thumb against her fingertips. "Money. Nathan figured his grandfather's modest lifestyle meant the money had to be in hiding."

"Which led him to Mrs. Bennett," Wally added.

Tammy shuddered. "He threatened his own great-aunt to keep quiet about what her brother had done."

"But Mrs. Bennett didn't know anything about the money," Xander said, exchanging glances with the others.

The rich aroma of brewing coffee entered the room as Mrs. Temperance carried mugs to the table. "Nathan became fixated on his grandfather's mumblings, believing if he listened long enough, Max would reveal everything."

Tammy stroked Lockie's fur as he wound between the chairs. "Without access to Max's ramblings, we're guessing Mary discovered Max's involvement with the heist and he sent the attic letter to keep her quiet." She sighed. "We're making a lot of assumptions."

Mrs. Temperance set a mug in front of Tammy and gave her a reassuring smile. "That's bound to happen with anything that occurred seventy years ago. Most everyone who knew the truth has passed on."

"The occupational hazard of working with a cold case, I guess," Tammy said, shifting in her seat before continuing their run-through. "Max confronts Mary at the little blue cottage and Eleanor sees him when she's out walking her dog."

"Mary refuses to leave town, so he kills her to guarantee her silence," said Wally.

"Victor interrupts him," said Tammy, "and Max has to hide. He locks the doors and remembers there was a cavity in the fireplace after working on the property with his father's construction company."

"He still has the weapon in his hand," Olivia faced the group, brandishing a knife with theatrical flair, "as he squeezes into the hole and replaces the stones."

"Once the sheriff leaves for the night, he creeps out and escapes through the field, disturbing Reg McLeod's sheep," added Xander.

"At home, with adrenaline pumping, he's pacing around the bedroom mumbling," Wally said as Olivia acted it out.

Mrs. Temperance pipes up, "Eleanor goes to the bathroom and hears him mention money and murder."

"Max discovers his sister saw him at the cottage and makes her lie to the sheriff to remove any suspicion of him," said Tammy. "And he gets away with murder."

"Seventy years later, he mumbles 'fireplace' to Nathan, who assumes the loot was in Tammy's house," said Wally.

"Which is why he tried to break in, coincidentally, the day I found the letter in the attic," said Tammy, "and again after trying to smother Mrs. Bennett."

"Did we know about that first break-in, dear?" said Mrs. Temperance with an eyebrow raised.

Olivia thumped the coffeepot on the table. Tammy noticed the flash of irritation in Olivia's eyes.

"Maybe not... sorry." Her cheeks grew hot. "I only figured out it was him after I recognized the Pac-Man T-shirt when he was arrested. It was also him at Mrs. Hubbard's Cupboard that day."

"What?" Xander's chair creaked as he jerked upright. "How do you know that?"

"Marjorie saw the pixelated ghost on the front of his T-shirt as he stormed toward her. A retro video game hero—a chomping yellow circle—was on the back, which I saw running away from my cottage."

Olivia plopped her hands on her hips. "You kept that clue to yourself."

"It was all so fragmented. I knew it was all important but I didn't know how or why. And then the sheriff arrived." *Oops. I probably should have told them about that.*

Wally thankfully changed the subject. "Nathan was arrested, Max died, and Mrs. Bennett tells all."

"And the seventy-year-old locked room murder of Mary Collins was solved," said a proud Mrs. Temperance.

Xander lifted his newly poured coffee. "To five amateur sleuths."

Lockie meowed as everyone raised their mugs.

"Okay. To *six* amateur sleuths solving the case," corrected Xander, patting Lockie's head.

*Can I finally go into my living room and make the cottage my home?*

# Chapter 28

One week later, Tammy, Olivia, Wally, Mrs. Temperance, and Xander made their way through the wrought-iron gates. Lockie trotted ahead, his tail high as he led the team through the winding paths between weathered headstones.

Tammy clutched a bouquet of white lilies, the cool petals brushing against her fingers. As they approached Mary Collins's final resting place, the weight of everything—the mystery, the friendships, the truth they'd uncovered—settled heavily in her heart. This wasn't about Mary anymore; it was about all of them.

Olivia walked beside her, cradling forget-me-nots. Behind them were Wally, Mrs. Temperance, and Xander.

As they rounded a corner, Tammy gasped. The simple plot, neglected for seventy years, was now buried beneath a sea of vibrant flowers—roses in pink and red, sunny daffodils, and purple irises mingled in a colorful tribute. Handwritten cards peeked out from the blooms, their edges fluttering with long-overdue remembrance.

"Oh my," Mrs. Temperance said, her eyes widening. "It seems we weren't the only ones who wanted to pay our respects."

The corners of Wally's mouth tugged up. "Looks like the whole town made sure Mary knows she's not forgotten."

They joined Mrs. Hubbard and another woman who placed pots of violets at the base of the grave.

"Afternoon," Mrs. Hubbard said, acknowledging them with a nod. "I see you've come to pay your respects as well."

Tammy was surprised by the usually reserved woman's presence. "We wanted to have a memorial for Mary. I never expected," she gestured to the floral tribute surrounding them, "all of this."

Mrs. Hubbard's lips twitched into a rare smile. "Mary Collins was before my time, I'm afraid." She turned to Mrs. Temperance. "When you shared Mary's story at last week's meeting..." she trailed off, pressing her lips together and shaking her head. "Well, some wrongs need righting, even if they're decades old."

The other woman stepped closer to Wally, touching his arm. "If this is what you do when I give you the archive's key, then it's yours any time you want it, flowers or no flowers."

Wally's eyes crinkled at the corners. "I'll hold you to that, Beverly. We couldn't have done it without that case file."

Beverly's cheeks flushed, and her eyes sparkled. "Did you hear that, Marjorie? I helped."

Mrs. Hubbard's response was equally soft but fierce. "We all did. After all, that's what Willowcroft does. We take care of our own, even if we were a bit late on this one."

Olivia knelt and placed her contribution among the display. "It's beautiful." Her eyes misted over.

Xander crouched beside her, lifting a card adorned with a hand-drawn sketch of the little blue cottage. "'To Mary, your story touched our hearts. May you rest in peace knowing the truth is finally known.' It's signed by the council."

Tammy's throat tightened as she surveyed the outpouring of love and re-membrance. She'd worried that Mary's story might have been forgotten, but the evidence before her proved otherwise. The people of Willowcroft had embraced Mary and were determined to honor her after so many years of mystery.

Mrs. Temperance dabbed at her eyes with a lace-edged handkerchief. "It's beautiful."

Wally placed a comforting hand on her shoulder. "It goes to show how much this case affected everyone. Mary might not have had any living relatives, but she's got a whole town behind her now."

Tammy set her lilies among the flowers. She took a deep breath, the mingled fragrances of the bouquets filled her lungs. "Mary, I walked into your cottage seeking refuge, not mystery. But you gave me both—a home and a purpose." She swallowed hard. "Look what you've done. Connected strangers, made them family. Showed us that buried truths refuse to stay hidden." The morning breeze swished through the cemetery's oak trees. "Your story's told now, Mary. And Willowcroft will remember."

Lockie padded over and sat beside the grave, his tail curled around his paws.

Wally clasped his hands in front of him. "Mary Collins, we stand here today to honor your life and to right a wrong that has persisted for far too long. As a former detective, I've seen my share of unsolved cases, but yours touched me in a way I never expected. Your story reminds us that justice, though sometimes delayed, should never be denied."

Olivia stepped forward, her glasses glinting in the sunlight. "Mary, as someone who loves books and stories, I want to assure you your tale will be remembered. It's become a part of Willowcroft's history, and we'll make sure it's told for generations to come."

Mrs. Temperance dabbed at her eyes again before speaking. "My dear, I was a child when you left us, but I've come to feel a bond with you through our investigation. Your spirit has touched us all, uniting this community in ways we never imagined."

Xander shuffled his feet and tugged at the hem of his T-shirt. "Um, hi Mary. I wanted to say that what happened to you wasn't fair. You deserved better. Your case taught me that history is more than dates in textbooks—it's real people with real stories. Thanks for that lesson."

As the group stood in silent reflection, a gentle draft rustled through the surrounding trees. Tammy closed her eyes, feeling a sense of peace wash over her. When she reopened them, she noticed Mrs. Hubbard wiping away a tear.

"Well," Mrs. Hubbard said, slightly hoarse, "I should be getting back. You all did right by Mary. The town won't forget that." She gave a curt nod. "Come on, Beverly, time to go." The two women turned and walked away.

"That was unexpected," Olivia said, following Mrs. Hubbard's retreating form. "I've never seen her show so much emotion."

Wally chuckled. "Sometimes it takes a tragedy to remind us of our shared humanity."

"It took me thirty years to peel back Marjorie's layers," said Mrs. Temperance. "And we'd known each other since kindergarten. Funny how saving the square's cobblestones cemented our friendship."

As they prepared to leave, a tugging sensation caught Tammy's leg. She looked down to see Lockie's green eyes fixed on something in the distance. Following his gaze, she spotted a familiar figure making her way slowly through the cemetery.

"Who's that?" Xander asked, squinting against the afternoon sun.

The elderly woman shuffled toward them, leaning heavily on a cane. Her face was etched with determination as she approached Mary's grave.

"Eleanor," Mrs. Temperance called out. "What a surprise to see you here."

Mrs. Bennett offered a wan smile as she reached the group. "I had to come." Her hands fidgeted with the strap of her handbag, and her breath hitched. "All these years... I've carried this burden. I owed it to Mary... and to myself."

Tammy moved to support Mrs. Bennett's other side, helping her closer to the grave. The older woman's eyes widened as she took in the sea of flowers and tributes.

"Oh my," she said. "I never imagined..."

"The whole town has united to honor Mary," Wally explained.

Tears welled in Mrs. Bennett's eyes. "After all these years... she deserves this." She fumbled in her pocket, pulling out a small, weathered envelope. With shaking hands, she placed it among the offerings.

"What's that?" Olivia asked.

"A letter," Mrs. Bennett replied. "One I should have written decades ago. It's an apology... and a promise to keep her memory alive."

Tammy's eyes misted over at the poignant gesture. She squeezed Mrs. Bennett's arm supportively. "I'm sure Mary would appreciate it."

As they stood there, a red cardinal alighted on Mary's headstone. Its bright plumage contrasted with the somber gathering. It tilted its head, observing the group before letting out a melodious trill.

Mrs. Temperance gasped. "Oh my! You know, they say when a cardinal appears, it's a visitor from heaven."

Xander's eyes widened. "Do you think it's Mary?"

Mrs. Bennett reached out a trembling hand toward the bird. "Is it you?"

It hopped closer, its red feathers gleaming in the afternoon sun. Its dark eyes locked with Mrs. Bennett's, delivering a message only she could hear. For a moment, the cemetery sat still; not a single leaf fluttered.

With its job done, the bird spread its wings, soaring over their heads and disappearing into the sky.

Mrs. Bennett exhaled a shaky breath. "I... I think she forgives me."

Tammy squeezed the older woman's arm. "Of course, she does. It's time to let it go."

Olivia nodded in agreement. "Mary's story is out now. Thanks to you, she can rest in peace."

As they made their way out of the cemetery, Tammy paused for one last look at Mary's grave. The flowers glowed in the late afternoon light, a testament to a life not forgotten. "Goodbye, Mary. And thank you."

Lockie meowed softly, as if adding his own farewell.

"So," Olivia said as they neared the gates, "what's next for our intrepid team of sleuths? Any more mysteries brewing in that cottage of yours, Tammy?"

Tammy laughed. "I think I've had enough real-life mysteries for a while. It's time to get back to writing fictional ones."

"Shame," Xander said with a grin. "I was getting used to being a detective."

"Well," Wally said, "there's always the mystery of who's been sneaking extra cookies from the jar at the senior center. We could use a young pair of eyes on that case."

Everyone chuckled, the somber mood lifting as they exited the cemetery.

# Chapter 29

Two weeks later, Tammy strolled toward the town square, the morning sun warming her face as Lockie trotted beside her. In LA, everyone drove everywhere. Here in Willowcroft, everything she needed was within walking distance—including her newfound family.

In a few weeks, her life had been transformed. In pursuit of peace, she instead found herself swept into a mystery that brought her so much more than she ever imagined: Wally, Mrs. Temperance, Olivia, Xander, and Lockie. Their shared adventure had restored her faith in friendship, teaching her to trust again.

A new novel poured out of her, fueled by their experiences, already half-finished. She smiled, quickening her pace toward their regular Saturday breakfast. Who would have thought solving a murder would mend her own heart?

"Lockie, can you believe how far we've come?" Tammy mused, glancing at her feline friend. He gave a contented purr. "Two strays finding a home."

Lockie paused to sniff a patch of clover before she nudged him with her foot. "Come on, buddy, we've got breakfast waiting."

As they entered the square, the newspaper stand caught her eye, the bold headline front and center. She bought one, slipped it under her arm and hurried to the diner.

The familiar tinkle of the bell and the sound of frying bacon welcomed her. The sizzle from the griddle was an invitation to relax. Her friends sat in their usual spot, each reading their own copy of the *Willowcroft Gazette*.

She slid into the booth next to Wally as she received curious glances from the other diners. An elderly couple raised their mugs toward her. "Good work, you all," the man said, tipping his hat. Tammy's cheeks warmed at the gesture. Her chest lifted briefly before she pushed back a loose strand of hair and slunk into the bench seat.

"Good morning!" she greeted her friends. "I see you all got an early start on the news today."

Wally chuckled, lowering his newspaper. "We made the front page!"

Tammy's grin spread as she smoothed out the paper. Her eyes locked onto the headline: "DNA Confirms Max Cross Killed Mary Collins in 1954." She traced the bold print with her fingertips. All the unanswered questions, all the long-buried secrets, had come to light.

DNA—from a fragment of preserved skin under the hilt of the knife—and fingerprints were discovered on the newly found murder weapon.

"Do you remember how I had to give fingerprint samples for elimination, since I was found holding the murder weapon?" Olivia said. "I was part of the inner workings of an official investigation."

Tammy divided her attention between the article and the lively chatter buzzing around her. Voices overlapped in the booth, each of them voracious in sharing their thoughts. Wally, ever the detective, focused on the sheriff's theory. "Makes sense that Max was protecting the money," he said while Xander devoured the details of the locked-room mystery. Tammy's bounding heart tried to absorb it all. Poor Mary. A young life cut short because she had been in the wrong place at the wrong time.

The article mentioned the hidden space behind the fireplace where they'd found the weapon, and how Max had hidden there instead of running.

"Was it really possible for Max to hide in there?" asked Xander. "It took a lot of effort for you to free that boulder, Wally."

"Max did it not long after it was built," said Wally. "There wasn't any mortar, just decades of dust and soot by the time I moved it. And remember, it was only a slice of a boulder. Besides, he only needed the big one in place initially. Victor would've been too focused on Mary's body to notice the fireplace, and the sheriff distracted by the body and witness, giving Max enough time to set the smaller stones. He'd killed Mary in a fit of rage—adrenaline and survival instinct surging. You can do a lot in that state."

"They mention us!" said Olivia.

"We are recognized for our detective skills." Mrs. Temperance chuckled as she sipped her tea.

"And they didn't forget our star sleuth." Tammy scratched Lockie behind his ears as his tail flicked.

"We've become quite the band of amateur sleuths," Wally remarked, a proud glint in his eyes as he reclined back in the booth.

A bold subheading caught Tammy's eye. "'Turn to page five for an exclusive with Nathan Cross.'"

"What could he possibly have to say?" Olivia said.

Everyone's pages crinkled. Wally reached the article first. "He agreed to a jail-house interview."

Xander adjusted his glasses. "Read it out loud, please."

Tammy cleared her throat. "'Nathan Cross, the grandson of Max Cross, accused of attempted murder of his great-aunt, revealed he was forced to drop out of college because the tuition fees weren't affordable. Nathan had to help pay bills to prevent his parents from losing their house. Believing his grandfather had hidden millions from the old bank heist, Nathan felt entitled to the money. He was determined to find it without implicating his grandfather in the crime.'"

Olivia pushed her coffee mug away. "He thought stealing was justified because he needed money?"

"Desperation can cloud judgment," Mrs. Temperance said, playing with a napkin.

"Like grandfather, like grandson." Wally jabbed at the paper. "Both were willing to do anything for wealth."

Olivia frowned. "He claims he wanted to protect his grandfather, yet his actions could have exposed everything."

"There's more," said Tammy. "According to a source close to the investigation, Nathan's mental state has deteriorated since the journalist's visit. In a bizarre twist, he's exhibiting behavior eerily reminiscent of his grandfather's final days."

Multiple mugs thumped on the table. "The source reports Nathan has taken to mumbling incoherently, much like Max Cross did in his last months. Guards have overheard him saying a string of unconnected words: 'fireplace,' 'blue cottage,' 'Mary,' and 'money.'"

Olivia leaned in. "History repeating itself."

Tammy's finger traced the lines of text. "Nathan appears fixated on the idea that the stolen money is hidden within the fireplace of the little blue cottage. However, the article points out the tragic irony of his delusion. The fireplace, as we now know, wasn't a hiding place for ill-gotten gains, but rather where Max concealed himself after committing the murder."

Mrs. Temperance's teacup rattled in its saucer. "Poor deluded boy."

"When informed that the murder weapon was found behind the fireplace stones, Nathan became even more agitated. He insisted the knife must have been placed there to 'guard the money' and they needed to 'dig deeper.'"

Wally let out a low whistle. "Sounds like he's lost touch with reality."

"The prison psychologist has recommended Nathan be transferred to a secure mental health facility for evaluation."

There was a moment of silence before Peggy approached with their breakfast. "Here we go, folks. A hearty meal for our town's mystery-solving squad!"

The familiar comfort of their usual Saturday routine lightened the mood until Xander said, "Have you seen the online comments? People are worried we're setting a dangerous example."

Their conversation halted as Sheriff Stanton strode in with the newspaper.

"Good morning. And congratulations. We couldn't have done it without you." He paused, turning serious. "However, investigations like this come with risks. Leave the heavy lifting to us."

Tammy understood the caution, but her chest swelled with immense satisfaction in their accomplishments.

"Of course, Stanton," Wally assured him. "We'll keep that in mind."

As the officer retreated to the counter, the team settled back into their breakfast and contemplation of the future. Tammy crunched on the crispy edge of her bacon, savoring the taste and the moment. Olivia drizzled maple syrup over a stack of fluffy pancakes, their conversation turning to what came next.

Xander's eyes sparkled as he declared this the best summer vacation ever, his youthful enthusiasm infectious. Olivia, her bookish demeanor softened by adventure, mused about adding genealogical crime-solving to her repertoire. Mrs. Temperance hinted at pursuing a more official volunteer role at the nursing home.

Tammy's gaze settled on Wally, his face alight as he proclaimed retirement the best decision he'd ever made. "Being able to use my skills without the constraints of protocol? It's liberating," he said, his words resonating with her own sense of newfound freedom.

In his jubilance, Xander had not absorbed Wally's potential change of heart regarding how things were done. Tammy suspected Wally would soon be right into Xander's tech.

This mystery had changed them all, and Willowcroft too.

As the group finished breakfast, a soft drizzle created a soothing rhythm on the diner's windows. Tammy breathed in deeply, feeling invigorated by the scent of fresh water mingling with pine.

"Ah, nothing like a little rain to add some atmosphere, huh?" Wally remarked, following her gaze out the window. "Makes you feel like we're in one of those classic detective novels."

Tammy chuckled. "Well, let's hope our next adventure is as memorable—but with less danger."

"Speak for yourself," Olivia said, closing her newspaper and tossing it onto the table. "I could use more adrenaline in my life."

Tammy shook her head, laughing. "You're going to get us all in trouble."

Olivia winked. "Curiosity killed the cat. But did you know, that information brought him back?"

As they stepped out of the diner, the soft patter of rain intensified, transforming the quaint town square into a glistening wonderland. Miniature waterfalls cascaded down the awnings of nearby shops.

"Looks like we need to make a dash for it," Mrs. Temperance said.

"It's only a summer shower, Mrs. Temperance," Olivia quipped, her eyes sparkling with mischief. She kicked off her shoes, letting out a delighted laugh as she twirled across the wet cobblestones. Her dress fanned out in the breeze, rain clinging to the fabric like tiny diamonds. Her burst of joy mingled with the pitter-patter on the pavement.

Unable to resist Olivia's infectious energy, Tammy kicked off her own shoes and joined the dance, letting the cool droplets splash against her skin and dampen her hair as they chased each other through the puddles.

Mrs. Temperance's silver bun glistened with raindrops as she swayed with Wally in slow steps. Xander tapped his feet to the rhythm of the shower.

Lockie observed from a nearby porch.

"Hey," Tammy called out, "let's make a promise that no matter what happens, we'll always be there for each other—through murder and mysteries." *And mothers.*

"Deal," they chimed in unison.

As they danced, Xander's voice broke through. "You know, they never found the money from the bank heist..."

Is the money still hidden in Willowcroft?
Read *Skeletons, Secrets & Speakeasies* to find out!
Find where to get your copy by scanning the QR code!

# BONUS Scene:

# Xander vs. The Willow-Crafters' First Group Chat

*(Mrs. Temperance's Living Room—Knitting Circle in Progress)*
**Attendance: Mrs. Hazel Temperance (a.k.a. Mrs. T), Mrs. Marjorie Hubbard, Mrs. Beatrice Smith, Mrs. Della Mae Beasley, Betty, and Xander.**

Xander didn't know how he'd gotten himself into this.

One minute, he was dropping off a package at Mrs. T's. The next, he was sitting in her floral armchair, surrounded by a brigade of grandmothers, trying to explain technology to people who still thought "the cloud" was just for rain.

Knitting needles clicked, the scent of freshly baked scones filled the air, and six pairs of expectant eyes stared at him like he was about to deliver the ultimate knitting hack.

Mrs. T, seated at her usual spot by the fireplace, smiled serenely as she poured tea. "Isn't this lovely, dear? A proper little lesson."

It was an ambush.

Betty, perched on the floral loveseat, beamed. "Oh, I just can't wait to be part of a real group chat! It's like we're in one of those spy movies! Secret messages and all."

Xander rubbed his temples. "It's... not exactly secret, Betty."

Marjorie, sitting stiffly in the wingback chair, adjusted her knitting needles. "I don't see the point in all this."

"You don't see the point," Mrs. Smith muttered, "but you're still here."

Marjorie ignored her.

Mrs. Beasley squinted at her phone, holding it as far away as possible, like she thought it might bite her. "Why is everything so small? How do you even read this?"

Betty leaned over. "Oh, Beasley, you can make the letters bigger! I do that for my romance books on my Kindle."

Xander raised an eyebrow. "You read romance on a Kindle?"

Betty winked. "You don't want to know the details."

Xander physically recoiled.

Mrs. T chuckled into her tea.

"Alright," Xander sighed. "Let's just get started." He held up his phone. "First, we're making a group chat. Everyone open your messages app."

There was a long pause.

Mrs. Beasley squinted. "Which one's that?"

Marjorie sighed dramatically. "It's the green one, Della Mae."

"Oh, dear. Mine's blue."

"That's Facebook."

"Oh."

Xander bit his lip to keep from laughing.

He walked them through it step by step, guiding them through creating a group and adding everyone's numbers.

"That's it," he said finally, "you're officially in a group chat."

The ladies stared at their screens in awe.

Mrs. Beasley tapped the keyboard. A second later, a single letter appeared.

**Della Mae:** H

**Marjorie:** What is that supposed to mean?

**Della Mae:** I don't know, I just pressed something.

Xander pinched the bridge of his nose.

**Beatrice:** Why did I get a text from myself?

Xander sighed. "That's just the chat showing you what you sent."

**Beatrice:** Oh. Well, that's unsettling.

**Betty:** HELLOOOOOOOOOOOO!!!

Xander winced. "Betty, your caps lock is on."

**Betty:** oops sorry!!

**Marjorie:** Why is there a thumbs-up button?

**Della Mae:** Oh, I do like that! How do I do one?

"Just hold down the message and tap the thumbs-up," instructed Xander.

**Betty:** Oh my, I found the heart!!!

**Marjorie:** Betty, stop hearting everything.

**Betty:** But it's so cute!

**Della Mae:** Where are the emojis? I want the one with the little dancing man.

Xander groaned into his hands.

**Beatrice:** Why does Betty's name have a picture next to it and mine doesn't?

"That's a profile picture. You can add one."

**Beatrice:** How?

"We'll do that another day."

Mrs. T, still serenely sipping her tea, finally sent a message.

**Hazel:** This is delightful. Thank you, dear.

Xander sighed in relief. At least one person appreciated the effort.

**Betty:** Oh look I found stickers!!!

Suddenly, the chat was flooded with animated hearts, dancing cats, and a winking teacup.

**Marjorie:** Betty.

**Betty:** What?? It's adorable!

**Della Mae:** I still want the dancing man.

Xander leaned back in his chair, exhausted. "This might be the most challenging thing I've ever done."

Mrs. T patted his hand. "Well, dear, now you know what it's like teaching a class. Perhaps we should start calling you Professor Xander."

Betty perked up. "Oh! That sounds very mysterious. Maybe you're training us for an underground crime-fighting league."

Marjorie rolled her eyes. "You've read too many novels, Betty."

Betty giggled and sent another flurry of hearts.

Mrs. T looked up from her knitting. "Oh, I do believe this is going to be very useful."

Marjorie, despite her earlier skepticism, gave a gruff nod. "Yes, I suppose it's... convenient."

**Betty:** We have to think of a name for our chat!

**Della Mae**: Oh, yes! Something sophisticated.

**Beatrice**: The Knitting Circle?

**Betty:** Boring!

**Marjorie:** We're not calling it Betty's Romance Club either.

**Betty:** Oh, but imagine! We could have book discussions and everything—

**Marjorie:** No.

**Hazel:** How about something fitting?

**Della Mae**: Spill the Tea & Purl?

**Hazel:** That's quite clever!

**Beatrice**: We don't always spill tea, Della Mae.

**Marjorie:** Speak for yourself.

**Betty:** Ooooh, what about The Loose Ends Society?!

**Della Mae**: That's actually quite good.

**Beatrice**: Fitting, considering we never finish our projects.

**Marjorie:** Some of us finish our projects, thank you very much.

**Betty:** Oh! What about The Knit-Wits?

**Marjorie:** Absolutely not.

Xander, rubbing his temples, sighed. "Okay, we need to settle this before I age another decade."

**Hazel:** How about we vote?

**Marjorie:** Oh, for heaven's sake.

**Betty:** Fine! But I get the final suggestion. What about... Knotty but Nice? A pause.

**Della Mae**: That's actually quite good.

**Beatrice**: It has a nice ring to it.

**Hazel:** Yes, I like that one.

**Betty:** Vote time! If you say yes, send a thumbs-up emoji!

A flurry of thumbs-up emojis flooded the chat.

"That was fast."

**Betty:** All in favor: Yes —except Marjorie.

**Marjorie:** This is ridiculous.

**Della Mae**: That's a yes from Marjorie.

**Marjorie:** That is NOT what I said!

**Betty:** Too late, it's official! Welcome to Knotty but Nice!

Mrs. T smiled warmly. "And just think, dear—now we can keep you updated on all the town's happenings."

Xander's stomach dropped.

**Marjorie:** Oh yes, now we can keep you in the loop, Xander.

**Betty:** Oh, I can send you all my book recommendations!!!

**Della Mae**: And pictures of my cat!

**Beatrice**: And knitting patterns!

Xander immediately regretted everything. "I've created monsters."

Mrs. T patted his arm. "What a wonderful idea this was."

Wait till you see what the Willow-Crafters get up to in Book Two!
To find out, get your copy of Skeletons, Secrets & Speakeasies here!

# Lockie, Leads & Loyalty

*Murder, Mystery & Mothers'* chapters written from Lockie the cat's perspective.

# Chapter 2

Ah, the war memorial fountain, my perfectly positioned surveillance post before *She* arrived. The water's constant babble provided excellent cover for my covert operations, including my professional people-watching activities. I could monitor everything: the humans with their laughably uncoordinated movements, the amateur squirrels attempting stealth (please), and the daily parade of potential subjects for investigation. My territory. My command center. Until Tammy appeared with Mrs. Temperance, changing everything with typical human disregard for established feline routines.

I first detected her presence by the fountain, her paws (hands, humans insist on calling them) moving about in that excessive way humans have when they communicate. Her scent story was fascinating, with traces of those noisy transport boxes humans love, leather seating (acceptable), and that distinctive nervous energy humans leak when they're uncertain. Yet something about this one stood out, a spark of potential that made my whiskers twitch with interest. Her eyes performed a surveillance sweep that would have impressed even the most discriminating cat—methodical and thorough, missing nothing. I deployed standard stealth protocols, utilizing the flower boxes for cover while conducting my preliminary assessment. This specimen warranted further investigation.

When she assumed the traditional human-offering-food position (at least she got that ritual right), I conducted a professional air analysis. Crackers. Not exactly premium fare, but her voice carried that special frequency, the one that suggests trainability. Her smile showed proper respect, free of the aggressive friendliness that sends any self-respecting cat running for cover. I took a precisely measured step forward, each paw landing without a sound, and accepted her tribute with dignity. Acceptable quality, all things considered. Then she had the audacity to assign me names: "Pawlock Holmes" and "Lockie." I narrowed my eyes at the presumption. The names did capture my essential brilliance, though I'd never admit it to her face.

She resumed her full height (humans and their obsession with vertical positioning) and exchanged verbal signals with Mrs. Temperance, who demonstrated unexpected wisdom by approving of my potential adoption of this human. Tammy then initiated the follow-me protocol. Naturally, I made it clear that any accompanying was entirely my decision. One must maintain standards. But something about her... intrigued my professional curiosity. She proceeded toward a blue cottage at the square's edge, and after conducting a thorough cost-benefit analysis, I permitted myself to escort her.

The cottage greeted us with essence of lemon (adequate cleaning protocols—promising). The space resonated with potential, as if it had been awaiting proper feline oversight. I conducted a comprehensive inspection: multiple premium sunbathing locations with excellent surveillance sight lines, a fireplace that practically begged for investigation (but that's another story), and satisfactory hiding spots for my future operations. My whiskers performed their standard space-assessment dance while I marked my territory. Yes, this establishment would serve admirably as my new headquarters. And Tammy? Well, as humans go, she showed remarkable promise as an assistant to my detective endeavors.

Little did I know then just how many mysteries awaited us in Willowcroft. But that's the thing about being a superior feline detective. You're always ready for the next case, even if your humans need a little time to catch up.

# Chapter 5

Mornings in my new command center showed potential. I'd strategically positioned myself on Tammy's feet during the night—optimal thermal benefits combined with prime surveillance opportunities. When she stirred, mumbling that typical human morning nonsense (as if they invented daylight), I bestowed upon her my perfectly executed slow blink. Just a gentle reminder of the natural order of things.

She performed her usual uncoordinated morning dance, those long human legs somehow managing to find the floor. I followed, obviously, but first treated myself to a thoroughly professional stretch sequence—back arched with textbook precision, each toe bean extended just so. As she gravitated toward the window (at least she's trainable), I claimed my observation post beside her. The sunbeam temporarily compromised my surveillance capabilities (note to self: adjust tactical positioning), but then movement. And not just any movement.

Some creature that could only be described as a walking disaster practically assaulted our gate, leaving a trail of botanical chaos in his wake. My tail immediately deployed its "situation-assessment" swish pattern. This specimen was fascinating, in a "what-in-the-nine-lives" sort of way.

His head fur resembled a dandelion caught in a windstorm (clearly never learned proper grooming), and that facial fur! You could cache a week's worth of mice in there. But the real puzzle was his choice of outer fur. A winter-weight coat in summer? Even the most tactically challenged cat knows better than that. The way it billowed behind him suggested he was going for dramatic effect, though his execution needed work.

Tammy pressed her nose against the glass like an amateur observer (we'll work on her technique later), concerned about him overheating. Honestly, humans and their misplaced priorities. My whiskers performed their full range of detection movements as I logged every detail of his suspicious behavior. His eye movements matched those of a cornered mouse, darting with desperation and clearly hiding something.

When Tammy asked who he was (as if I'd share intelligence that easily), I gave her my patented "obviously-suspicious-activity-in-progress" look. Naturally, it went right over her head. Humans can be disappointingly slow on the uptake.

She dismissed it as small-town quirkiness (amateur assessment) and finally remembered her primary morning duty: feeding me. I executed my standard weaving maneuver through her legs as she moved about—part guidance, part reminder of proper priorities. When breakfast finally arrived (we'll need to work on her timing), I demonstrated appropriate enthusiasm for her benefit. One must encourage good behavior in one's humans.

"Whoa there, tiger," she laughed, clearly impressed by my dining technique. Tiger? Please. I'm a panther in disguise, operating undercover in domestic cat form. I adjusted my consumption speed slightly—purely to humor her, mind you. She rewarded me with adequate ear scratches before attending to her own significantly less interesting meal.

Sometimes I wonder if humans realize just how much work goes into training them properly. But Tammy showed promise. With time and proper feline guidance, she might just develop into a decent assistant for my investigative endeavors. Though clearly, we had our work cut out for us with this coat-wearing mystery human.

Get the full version as a gift
when you sign up to my newsletter.

**"Lockie, Leads & Loyalty"— The Mary Collins Investigation as told by Lockie the cat.**

Discover what Lockie really thinks about being adopted by Tammy and her detective skills.

**Get your copy now!**

Visit: https://dl.bookfunnel.com/sfc832tpz8
OR scan the QR code

Newsletter subscribers get behind-the-scenes content, exclusive bonus material, puzzles, and more!
*I respect your privacy and will never share your information. You can unsubscribe at anytime.*

# YOUR THOUGHTS MATTER!

Did you enjoy Murder, Mystery & Mothers? Your honest review helps other readers find it.

## Where to Leave Your Review:

### Amazon:

### Goodreads:

QUICK TIP: Even one sentence about what you enjoyed makes a difference!

Thank you for helping other readers discover this story.

```
Y C T P T A M M Y M Y R Y E
M I E Y W B E R R W A E R F
U T T M N F N E O E O X A I
R T T Y I A N A G L T L M R
D A A N H E Y L L A W T W E
E N K T N Y I R T O T Y E P
R M A C U I P K E E I T E L
B N I A T C G H C D L E O A
E S Y I N C H L E O N B H C
N C O T A R O E T I L A M E
N C R O S S U C G S I X O
E H I M Y S T E R Y E T E H
T M L F E U L C L R S F E D
T T E R C E S L I B R A R Y
```

## Murder, Mystery & Mothers
By Frances Heap

| | |
|---|---|
| Attic | Lockie |
| Bennett | Mary |
| Clue | Max |
| Cottage | Murder |
| Cross | Mystery |
| Fireplace | Nathan |
| Ghost | Secret |
| Heist | Tammy |
| Knife | Wally |
| Letter | Xander |
| Library | |

```
M E H O S B A S K E R V I L L E S
E L O I N V E S T I G A T E I A M
U R A Y Y S K E T E Y L E N D O I
O C E D B R T E T E E R E O R N N
I O B M V T L E A I T S E I N D S
N C A E I E T G N S I P A T O L E
O Y K P V R N L Y U I R O C S E L
I D E O E I C T G P T E R U T Y E
T E R V D M D S U Y E T D D A B M
U T S I U L I E L R Y L U E W H E
L E T L T D G R N O E T I D O T N
O C R L I M O C M C N T C L I T T
S T E A E L T L E U E D M S E E A
R I E I L D T U L R R E O T D I R
I V T N M D A E R O S D D N E M Y
E E G N I Y F I N G A M E I V R C
D R A Y D N A L T O C S L R E V E
```

## Sherlock Holmes
By Frances Heap

| | |
|---|---|
| ADVENTURE | INVESTIGATE |
| BAKERSTREET | LONDON |
| BASKERVILLES | MAGNIFYING |
| CLUE | MORIARTY |
| CRIME | MURDER |
| DEDUCTION | MYSTERY |
| DETECTIVE | PIPE |
| DISGUISE | SCOTLANDYARD |
| ELEMENTARY | SOLUTION |
| EVIDENCE | VILLAIN |
| HOLMES | WATSON |

For more puzzles

**(crosswords, jigsaws, mini mysteries, word searches and wordles)**

head to my website:

https://franheapwriter.com/puzzles/

Fran, currently living in Melbourne, Australia, has wanted to be a writer since she was nine. It only took her forty years to get there! With two travel books written to test the waters she is now writing cozy mysteries and having a fabulous time doing so. She has no intention of stopping with multiple series planned and begun.

Before her writing life she travelled the world while working as a nanny and neonatal nurse. She has visited 61 countries but aims to visit over 190.

By her own admission, she's a terrible redhead with a penchant for quirky data collecting and thinking outside the box. Her favourite motto is "Curiosity killed the cat, *but information brought her back.*" There is a lot of Fran in Olivia, but also in Tammy too. She loves ancient ruins and drains, hates dusting, loves going behind the scenes, can't smile in photos and detests selfie sticks. In her younger days, she wanted to be an actress, an astronaut, a hostel owner, a department store owner, a doctor and a writer.

When she was ten, she wrote in her diary: *Tonight I vowed I will get a story published at some stage before I die.*